THE MESSAGE
FOR T...

Someone w... ...wn of
Gidding. T... ...mur-
dered, their ... ...Tarot
cards.

Could the killer be the wealthy racehorse owner
with a guilty secret . . . the ambitious social
climber who knew too much . . . the charming
student who outsmarted his professors . . . the
arrogant clairvoyant who *had* to be right?

The exceptional Mrs. Charles knew that someone was playing with dangerous forces. She
would summon all her powers to solve the Tarot
murders . . . even if the next card was meant
for her.

. . . WAS MURDER!

MURDER INC.® MYSTERIES

SCENE OF THE CRIME™ MYSTERIES

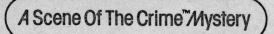

A Scene Of The Crime™ Mystery

THE TAROT MURDERS

Mignon Warner

A DELL BOOK

Published by
Dell Publishing Co., Inc.
1 Dag Hammarskjold Plaza
New York, New York 10017

Dell ® TM 681510, Dell Publishing Co., Inc.

ISBN: 0-440-16162-2

Reprinted by arrangement with
David McKay Company, Inc.-Ives Washburn, Inc.

Printed in the United States of America

First Dell printing—March 1981

CONTENTS

AUTHOR'S NOTE

The seventy-eight cards in the standard Tarot deck are divided into two packs known as the Major Arcana and Minor (or Lesser) Arcana, and it is with the first of these, the Major Arcana, that this book is concerned, its twenty-two chapters representing the twenty-two symbolic picture cards in that pack.

The brief interpretations of the meanings of each of these picture cards in relation to their corresponding chapters, and the various other readings of the Tarot throughout the book, are based on my own personal knowledge and understanding of the Tarot.

PROLOGUE

Mrs. Charles opened The Bungalow's front door hesitantly. One seldom received unexpected callers at this
hour of night, and she did not recognise the pale,
hollow-eyed young woman who had knocked so loudly
and insistently. In the momentary pause before anyone spoke, it flashed through Mrs. Charles' mind that
the girl had probably left the motorway by the wrong
exit and was now lost and seeking directions, either
into the village proper or to Gidding or to wherever
else it may be that she was journeying so very late at
night.

The girl took advantage of Mrs. Charles' hesitancy
and spoke first.

"Madame Herrmann?" The query in the girl's voice
was sharp and tense. She faltered, glancing nervously
round the somewhat mystified, middle-aged woman
standing before her into the shadowy hall where a
grandmother-clock was striking the half-hour after
midnight. Looking back at Mrs. Charles, she then
frowned and said, "Madame Adele Herrmann, *the
clairvoyante?*"

Mrs. Charles' deep blue eyes searched the girl's face
carefully, trying to place it. *Did she know this young
person?* She thought not. The girl was too young . . .
she could be little more than eighteen or nineteen,
twenty at most, and it was a long time ago now—more
than a decade—since the halcyon days of the booth
on the pier. *London, perhaps?* No, even that was some
while in the past, and again the girl would have been

much too young to have consulted a clairvoyant, though there was always the possibility that a member of her family had been a client at one time or another. . . .

The blue eyes narrowed shrewdly. Never mind how the young woman knew about *Madame Herrmann*. There were far more serious considerations . . . This girl was in trouble, frightened and distressed.

"Yes," said Mrs. Charles quietly. "I am Adele Herrmann. How can I help you?"

The girl moistened her bottom lip which was very dry—cracked, Mrs. Charles noted. The girl also had very beautiful eyes, an unusual, deep violet colour, blurred and magnified through the tears which suddenly filled them and splashed down her colourless cheeks. Momentarily, her chin dimpled and wrinkled as the muscles of her throat tightened and became taut with emotion. Then, in a strangulated whisper, she said, *"I am going to die."*

The expression on Mrs. Charles' face became intently thoughtful. The young woman certainly looked far from well, but usually it was to the medical profession or to the church, perhaps to a spirit healer, that one turned for help and succour when one's health threatened one's continued existence. There was, in Mrs. Charles' *(Madame Adele Herrmann's)* experience, only the one kind of threat to a person's life that brought him or her to the clairvoyant's door-step, hoping—as Mrs. Charles had no doubt that this young woman hoped—that the clairvoyant would pick up some kind of mystic magic wand and then, pointing it heavenwards, make all the bad things which were tormenting her go away and leave her in peace.

Very quietly, Mrs. Charles said, "We are all going

to die, child. One day. In your case, I shouldn't
wonder that that event will occur very much later
rather than sooner."

The girl looked at her strangely. "But the Professor said the cards never lie."

"The cards?" Mrs. Charles' eyebrows rose fractionally. "The Tarot?"

The girl's eyes widened with fear. Her tears evapo-
rated. "He said it would be soon, very soon. Tonight,
even. . . ."

"Come," said Mrs. Charles, stepping back from the
door with a warm, inviting smile. "Let me make you
a cup of tea and then while you're drinking it, you
can tell me what troubles you."

The girl stiffened. *"No!"* she said sharply. Her face
began to twitch and her head jerked spasmodically
round to the left as if by some kind of choreiform
movement or nervous tic over which she had no
direct control. "There isn't time. It's too late."

"You don't really believe that or you wouldn't have
come to me seeking my help," said Mrs. Charles gently.

"Oh, you can't help me. No one can help me!" the
girl cried out distractedly. "I don't know what I'm
doing here, why I came. It was stupid. It's too late.
. . ." She moved away from the door. As she turned,
a faint odour from either her clothing or her person—
neither pleasant nor unpleasant—wafted over Mrs.
Charles, vividly rejuvenating the faded memory of a
particularly happy summer during her childhood spent
on a large agricultural estate in Scotland.

"This person you called 'the Professor' . . ." Mrs.
Charles began. She spoke slowly and thoughtfully, as
though talking to herself. "He made the prediction
of death from a reading of the Tarot?"

The girl paused at the sound of the older woman's voice and turned. She stood motionless and stared at Mrs. Charles vacantly, as if she hadn't heard what had been said to her. Then, after a very long moment, she shook her head and said, "No. I took the card to him and he told me what it meant, what was going to happen to me."

"What card was that, child?" asked Mrs. Charles, her voice gentle, persuasive.

The girl seemed not to understand.

"There are many cards in the Tarot which may, in certain circumstances, predict death, my dear," the clairvoyante went on. "Some more powerful and evil than others. Which card was it that you showed to your friend . . . to the Professor?"

The girl's mouth started to work but no sound came out. Then, moistening her lips and with an effort, she said, simply, "Justice. *Justice!*" she repeated loudly, in an unexpected flash of anger, when the clairvoyante failed to respond.

"But child," said Mrs. Charles imperturbably. "That cannot be: it isn't possible. No one single card from the Major Arcana of the Tarot, to which that card, *Justice,* belongs, can predict such a thing: not with anything like the degree of certainty which you have attributed to it. I am both astonished and dismayed that anyone should proffer such a rash, irresponsible prediction with so little—in fact, or so it would seem, with not the slightest shred of substantiating evidence. . . ." The shrewd eyes narrowed. "That is if I have understood you correctly and there was but the one solitary card in the reading."

The girl's dry, bloodless lips were drawn back over her small, even white teeth in a tight, bitter little smile. "It's true, isn't it? I can tell by the look on your face. I *am* going to die," she said in a thin, rasping voice.

Mrs. Charles looked deep into the girl's eyes. There had been defiance in the voice, and yet the pleading in the eyes was unmistakable. The girl believed implicitly what 'the Professor' had told her, but she was beseeching her—begging with what little hope there was left in her poor tormented mind, thought Mrs. Charles —to make it not so.

"*Justice!*" The girl's voice was harsh, the line of her jaw hard and unyielding. Then, suddenly, her whole body shuddered convulsively from head to toe and she started to laugh. It was a jarring, discordant sound which, after a few disturbing moments, was caught up in a loud single sob. "*Thou shalt not kill!* Thou shalt not *be* killed . . . *be* killed *be* killed," she chanted softly, almost to herself. Her head was averted and her eyes stared vacantly over her left shoulder into the very still darkness beyond the road which had brought her from the motorway to the clairvoyante's isolated bungalow.

"Have you killed someone, child? Is that why you fear justice so?"

The girl's head jerked round to the front and she gave Mrs. Charles an odd look. "Me? Have *I* killed someone?" She thought for a full minute before answering. "I can't remember," she said at length, shaking her head slowly. There was a bewildered expression on her face, as if not being able to remember were something of a shock to her. "I might have," she admitted. "A long time ago." She paused and reconsidered the possibility, all the while staring hard at Mrs. Charles without seeing her. After a minute or two, her brow furrowed. "You're confusing me. *I'm* the one who is going to be killed. The card said so."

"For you to be so sure of that card's meaning, there must have been other far more powerful cards in the reading that was done for you of the Tarot." The clairvoyante spoke quietly but insistently. "Believe me, child," she went on, the subtle change in her tone of voice taking on greater emphasis and sounding very definite, "that card, alone, cannot make such a prediction. You are misguidedly attributing to it powers which it simply does not possess. Not by any stretch of the imagination—"

"*Stop!*" the girl cried out. She screwed up her eyes and covered her ears with her hands. "I don't want to talk about it any more. I shouldn't have come. It's written . . ."

"Nothing is *written*, child," said Mrs. Charles firmly. "There is little that cannot be changed if one's desire for change is sincere enough. With the exception, perhaps, of one's health. But there is nothing wrong in that direction is there, my dear? That is not what troubles you. Nor, I believe, is it the card from the Tarot. That—*Justice*—is merely the symbol of your fear. What or who threatens your life, child? Why do you fear justice?"

Another strange, highly disturbing expression crossed the girl's face. Her hands slipped slowly from her ears and came to rest under her chin. "He says I know, but I don't . . . *really* I don't."

"*Who* says you know?"

The girl did not answer immediately. Nervously, she fingered the tiny capital letter *M* on the fine gold chain round her neck. Her finger-nails, Mrs. Charles observed, were badly bitten and her hands generally work roughened and calloused.

"*He*," the girl repeated. "He says it's all there locked up in my subconscious and that I'm deliberately keeping it there because I lack the courage to face the truth. He says I don't *want* to remember. But I *can't*: I've tried and I can't!"

"Let me help you, child. Permit me to read the Tarot for you."

"*No!*" the girl said sharply. "He said I mustn't let you look at the cards for me. He said I wasn't to trust you."

Again something stirred in Mrs. Charles' memory, this time something unpleasant which she would rather had remained well and truly forgotten. "This person you referred to as '*the Professor*'," she began hesitantly. "Do I know him? What is his name?"

The girl threw back her head and started to laugh. "*Professor?*" she said, choking a little on her laughter. "Professor . . . yes—*ha ha ha!*—that's a good name for him. *Professor Tarot!*" Still laughing, she backed away and within seconds was lost to Mrs. Charles in the velvety blackness of the warm summer's night.

Meditatively, the clairvoyante closed the door. The girl's laughter echoed hollowly in her ears.

Excerpt from a front page news item in the *Gidding Daily Sketch* of the 17th August . . .

"*The body of a young woman discovered early last Sunday morning in the shallows off Beacon Point has now been positively identified as that of Lorna Maude Lock, the younger daughter of the distinguished Harley Street psychiatrist, Mr. S. J. Lock. The dead girl, a twenty-year-old university student, was spending the summer vacation working locally as a stable-hand for the prominent racing horse owner/trainer, Mr. Amery Walters. The Gidding police have as yet declined to make any official comment with regard to the girl's death, but it is widely expected that some form of public statement will be made within the next twenty-four hours either confirming or denying the current spate of speculation that the dead girl was the second victim of the so-called 'Tarot Murderer'. . . ."*

A Person of Singular Individuality

"Superintendent! how nice to see you: do come in."

Mrs. Charles smiled warmly at her visitor. "You are looking very fit and well: the long hot summer is agreeing with you."

"And with you, too, Madame," responded David Sayer solemnly.

The clairvoyante smiled to herself at the *'Madame'*. He had addressed her thus over the telephone that afternoon . . . a sure sign that he was on 'official' business and about to ask a favour of her. The *'Madame'* kept everything on a strictly business basis and gave her the right—or so she believed she was correct in thinking—to refuse his request without the risk of his taking offence and there being some harm done to their personal relationship with one another.

As they went through to the sitting-room, Mrs. Charles asked politely after his family, and he responded in kind with an enquiry about her brother.

"There didn't appear to be any sign of life about when I drove past his house a few minutes ago," he went on. "Mr. Forbes isn't ill, I hope."

"Cyril's visiting a friend down at the seaside for a few days," explained Mrs. Charles. "I've only just returned from a holiday trip abroad myself."

David glanceed round the pleasant, unobtrusively furnished room and then made himself comfortable in the imitation mid-Victorian button-backed leather armchair near the open fireplace which somehow seemed to him to be the piece of furniture most suited to his mission.

"Can I offer you something to drink, Superintendent?" the clairvoyante went straight on. "Tea? Something stronger, perhaps?"

The ex-Detective Chief Superintendent of Police shook his head. "Thank you, no."

Mrs. Charles sat down opposite him on the sofa and folded her hands in her lap. A handsome woman with strong, determined features and short, feathery gold hair, her sole concession to the eccentricities which most people expect of someone in her profession was her passion for what some would call excessively showy diamond rings which she indulged in the extreme. David couldn't resist a fleeting smile as his eyes lighted upon the little finger of her left hand, the only digit without a jewelled adornment of any kind (he counted nine rings in all, but was prepared to admit that he might have missed the odd one or two here and there), and wondered what it had done to deserves such markedly shabby treatment.

"It was kind of you to agree to see me like this, Madame . . . at such short notice," he began stiffly. "I only wish that the circumstances of my visit were less unpleasant. Once again it is to confer with you about murder, two murders—"

"I hope not history repeating itself, Superintendent," she remarked with a thoughtful smile, recalling that time, not so very long ago, when he had made a similar semi-official visit to her bungalow to discuss a double murder mystery.

"Please don't misunderstand me," he said quickly. "It is not to accuse *you* of murder that I have come to see you this time, Madame. Rather, it is to ask for your help . . . Madame Adele Herrmann's help."

Mrs. Charles made no comment. The blue eyes regarded him solemnly.

His mouth twisted into a wry smile. "I carry two briefs—one, curiosity (my own), and the other . . ." He hesitated. "The other is on behalf of two of my closest friends, James and Mary Sutherland."

"Mr. Sutherland . . . the veterinary surgeon?" asked Mrs. Charles, surprised.

"Yes," he replied. "It is the Sutherlands' request, and because they are such close friends, that I've taken the liberty of approaching you and asking for your help."

He paused, but characteristically, Mrs. Charles made no comment and simply waited patiently for him to continue.

"They," he went on, "James and Mary, are deeply concerned about a godson of theirs who has found himself rather unfortunately—and quite innocently, I might add," he said with a quick frown, "involved in murder. You are familiar, are you not, with the so-called Tarot murders?"

The blue eyes widened. "The Tarot murders? No, Superintendent: I can't say that I am."

He looked puzzled: then, abruptly, his face cleared. "Of course not," he said quickly. "You said you've been abroad: you were obviously away at the time of the publicity over the second Tarot murder, which is when the murders were first tagged with that label by the Press. And to be perfectly frank with you, Madame, the Gidding police have since been trying to keep the whole business as low-key as possible, largely to avoid public hysteria—the last thing the police want is everyone in and around Gidding getting the idea into their heads that there could be a homicidal maniac on the loose in their midst—and also because of the, er, *difficult* nature of this kind of murder . . . any crime with occult overtones. Ignoring the phone calls, the Gidding police have so far received over a hundred *written* offers to help to solve the Tarot murders, either per medium of the crystal ball or the Tarot itself—one old dear even turned up at police headquarters with her crystal ball snugly tucked up in her knitting hold-all, ready to get cracking on the case. And in addition, there have been something like twelve *full* confessions to the crimes—that's almost a confession a day since the last murder was committed."

He paused and sighed. "I am afraid that this kind of murder investigation is pure hell for the police. Every nutcase who has ever played about with the Tarot or a crystal ball—" He broke off and looked extremely embarrassed. "You'll forgive me, Madame," he said swiftly. "I meant nothing personal. I was merely generalising."

"I understand perfectly, Superintendent," said the clairvoyante with a faintly amused smile. "Please continue: I find all of this most intriguing."

"I'll start at the beginning," he said, and she nodded her acquiescence.

"Seven weeks ago, on the morning of Sunday the Eleventh of July, a young trainee nurse was found murdered—brutally battered and bruised about the face and head, then strangled to death—in a ditch roughly midway between her parents' home in Hetley Vale (a small market town north-west of Gidding)," he explained abruptly, "and Gidding itself. The dead girl was doing her training at Gidding General, but was on sick leave at the time of the murder and had gone home to her parents for a rest. Mr. and Mrs. Noad —the girl's parents (her name was Miriam, by the way)—told the police that on the night she was murdered, Miriam left home at about eight thirty to attend a fairly popular night-spot—popular, that is, with her age group, of course . . . a place called The Black Cat Disco, which is less than a mile from her parents' home. There's a bit of a parking problem in the town centre—where the disco is situated—and so the girl declined her father's offer of the loan of his car for the evening, and set off on foot.

"She never reached her destination. Approximately one and a half hours later, somewhere shortly after ten that night, she was murdered. Her body was dumped—pushed down a fairly steep embankment into the ditch where it was ultimately discovered early the following morning, on the Sunday—possibly from a moving car. It rained very heavily that night between two a.m. and seven thirty which had the effect of wiping the whole area clean as a slate. The police found only one clue—and I use the word 'found' very loosely in this instance because the murderer deliberately left it for them to find. A Tarot card. The one called *The Star*."

Mrs. Charles nodded thoughtfully. "The police are quite certain that the girl's murderer left the card from the Tarot for them to find . . . it couldn't have been hers?"

"No. The police checked that out with her family and friends all of whom seemed quite definite that she didn't own a pack of Tarot cards, or know anything about the Tarot."

"Had she ever consulted a clairvoyant?"

"No, she wasn't that type."

Mrs. Charles concealed a smile. The Superintendent was sometimes really quite amusingly inept at concealing his little prejudices.

"I see," she said slowly. "Please continue."

"No queries about the Tarot card?" he asked, a trifle surprised and disappointed at her apparent lack of interest in it.

"Only one, but it can wait for the moment. It's better that I hear you out, then I shall ask my questions."

He nodded and then went on:

"The killer left the Tarot card on the dead girl's chest beneath her arms which he crossed over the card."

He demonstrated the pose, crossing his arms on his chest with his hands pointing toward his shoulders, and Mrs. Charles nodded slowly.

"So at some time," she said, "the killer left his car—if the dead girl was pushed from it while it was moving, as you've suggested might have been the case—and then followed after her down the embankment into the ditch to arrange her body in the manner in which he wished it to be discovered."

"Yes. A car parked near the embankment might've leaked oil or left behind some other tell-tale evidence, so the police think he pushed her body out of the car while it was mobile (she might not have even rolled down into the ditch at that juncture, he might've taken care of that later): then he drove on, probably stopped somewhere off the road—left his car parked some considerable distance away from the embankment, I should imagine—and then returned and did what he had, or wanted, to do with the body.

"Whichever way it was, one thing is for certain. He's a callous, cold-hearted devil . . . at least, that's how I picture him. Most of the murders which came within my range of experience as a police officer could justifiably be called crimes of passion, family squabbles in the main; and while murder can never be condoned, no matter what the circumstances, only a hypocrite would pretend that there aren't instances where some poor wretches are driven to it, and likewise pretend not to understand the underlying passions which lead up to their crimes. But in the case of the Tarot murderer—" he shook his head slowly "—no, I don't think so. This man kills in cold blood, without feeling a thing. Miriam Noad was an exceptionally pretty girl . . . that is, before her path and the Tarot murderer's crossed," he said, grim-faced. "She was very popular, happy-natured, fun-loving, kind-hearted, deadly serious about her nursing career to which she was totally dedicated—there was no special one young man in her life—and everyone . . . her tutors, her family and friends insist that she was highly intelligent and an extremely sensible, thoroughly responsible young person."

"Not the kind of girl to accept a lift in a car with a total stranger or to court cheap thrills," said Mrs. Charles absently.

"No," he said grimly. "So there you have it: Tarot murder No. 1. No motive. No suspects. Nothing but a very slight theory that Miriam Noad might've, only *might've*, accepted a lift with a stranger who was prowling the streets of Hetley Vale in his car that

Saturday night looking for a victim to satisfy his in-
sane lust for killing . . . a homicidal maniac who
chooses his victims without rhyme or reason and kills
for the sake of killing."

Mrs. Charles gave David a keen look. Why, she wondered, should the Superintendent be so sure that there was no rhyme or reason to the Tarot murderer's selection of his victims? Was that a personal opinion, or was he reflecting both his own attitude and that of the Gidding police to the Tarot murders? And if so, what had led them to draw that very curious conclusion about the Tarot murderer . . . their inside knowledge of similar crimes and of the persons who had committed them? Or was there some other overriding influence? A sudden, startling thought occurred to her. These assumptions about the Tarot murderer weren't based on the Tarot card that he had left with his victim? The police would undoubtedly have got someone to interpret *The Star* for them, and surely that person would know what he or she was talking about. . . .

"Now," David went on, abruptly terminating the clairvoyante's ponderings, "moving forward five weeks, we come to Tarot murder No. 2. Victim: Lorna Lock. A university student—going for an arts degree . . . that's if she'd stayed the distance, which those who knew her best doubted. She had the brains, but was flighty—couldn't be bothered applying herself to her studies or to anything much, it seems. Well-off. Her father is a Harley Street psychiatrist. Like a lot of his kind," he commented, a shade bitterly, "can sort out other people's problems, but makes one hell of a mess of his own. He and the girl didn't get along. The

mother died some years ago, which is roughly when—
or so it would appear—daughter Lorna started running off the rails. She had a reputation for being wild
and something of a nuisance. Nobody seemed to like
her much, if at all, and the more aware she was of a
person's dislike for her, the bigger pest she made of
herself in that quarter."

"How very sad," murmured Mrs. Charles.

David hesitated and considered her remark. "Yes,"
he said at length, "I suppose it was. Anyway, she
wangled herself a job during the long summer vacation with Amery Walters."

"The racehorse trainer?"

"Yes. And when I say wangled, I mean wangled!
Her father's closest friend owns Little Eva—" He
raised his eyebrows interrogatively. "The horsy super-
star who picked up over £80,000 in prize-money at
Ascot and is now hot favourite for the Arc de Tri-
omphe in October?"

Mrs. Charles nodded her head to indicate that she
had heard of the filly which sports writers and com-
mentators alike referred to as 'the all-time wonder
horse'.

David continued:

"Little Eva's owner more or less insisted that Lorna
should be given a job and Walters, who was in no
position to refuse to play ball, was obliged to take the
girl on despite howls of protest from his son, Peter.
Peter Walters is a student at the same university—the
one the girl used to attend—and the two of them had
been at loggerheads ever since she'd reduced a serious
play which he had written and then co-produced with
a friend of his at the university, to the levels of a

French farce. She auditioned for a part in the play and although others had turned in a far better performance, it was decided to give her the part rather than risk the consequences of a refusal. She had a reputation for being particularly vindictive towards anyone who said 'no' to her, and I think I would be right in saying that people were quite frightened of her, of this vindictive, self-destructive streak in her nature. Anyway, Peter Walters' play ended up a riot and she made a complete ass of him. Then, still smarting from this humiliation, young Walters comes home for the summer holidays only to find that Daddy has taken on his tormentor, Little Miss Self-Destructive, as a stable-hand."

"Dear me," murmured Mrs. Charles.

"Once Walters had explained his position to his son, the boy accepted the situation in a very adult fashion apparently, and simply ignored the girl. Which, by all accounts, drove her right round the bend. And almost everybody else at the stables, I understand. Her childish, undisciplined behaviour, pranks—stupid practical jokes—at Peter Walters' expense for the most part, pushed everyone to the point of desperation. Tempers were becoming frayed, discipline was shot to pieces. . . ."

"With horses as valuable as Little Eva entrusted to his care, Amery Walters must have been a very anxious man," she commented.

He agreed. "James—James Sutherland—said the wrong sort of rumours were starting to get around, and more than one owner had been over to have a serious talk with Walters about them, and to see for themselves what was going on. However, that is all by the by . . . The girl, Lorna Lock, was thought to have been staying in digs somewhere in Gidding—the police don't know exactly where yet."

He shrugged a little. "She was certainly a wild one . . . a real will-o'-the wisp, anti-social to a fault! Would sleep rough, out in the open in all weathers, if the mood took her. Nobody can recall ever having seen her actually sitting down to eat a meal of any kind. She didn't seem to need food. She used to hitch-hike from Gidding out to Walters' place around six in the morning. She didn't own or drive a car. Her mother died following an accident which occurred while she (the mother) was giving Lorna a driving lesson—no one's fault, really . . . just one of those freak accidents that sometimes happen. I don't know the full details, but I believe the Lock family—there's another daughter a few years older than Lorna—were holidaying on one of the smaller Greek islands at the time: Mrs. Lock and Lorna were driving alone along a narrow mountain road and for some unknown reason, the girl, who was at the wheel, panicked and lost control of the car and they went hurtling over the edge. Mrs. Lock was critically injured, though it was some little while afterwards that she actually died from her injuries.

"But getting back to the girl's job with Walters . . . Her main duties were mucking out the horse-boxes and keeping the yard clean. Not surprisingly, Walters drew the line at letting her handle or ride any of his prized horseflesh, even though she was an expert horsewoman. Walters made this discovery after she defied his instructions and took Little Eva out of her box while no one was about. No harm came to the horse, but thereafter Walters didn't take any more chances and put a round the clock watch on the stables. Then for a few days after the Little Eva incident, all was peace and quiet. Walters says that the girl seemed to be a completely different person—arrived punctually for work in the morning, got on with her job, had practically nothing to say to anyone . . . completely ignored Peter Walters: then, at the end of each day— somewhere around seven in the evening, usually—she quietly set off back to her digs.

"This short period of calm," he interpolated with a quick frown, "immediately preceded Saturday, August Fourteen . . . she was murdered during the early hours of Sunday the Fifteenth, two weeks ago today. Then, all of a sudden, on that Saturday—the Fourteenth—she started playing up again: there was an incident early in the day which caused quite a bit of alarm at the time, and then late in the evening, she was caught red-handed in one of the horse-boxes by the stable-hand who was on guard duty. This was sometime after eleven, a good four hours after she'd been seen walking down the lane towards the bus stop. The stable-hand dragged her off up to the house and she and Walters had a blazing row. In the finish, Walters threw her out . . . told her to get off his property and not to come back."

"Mr. Walters decided to risk the displeasure of her father's friend?"

"Apparently so. Walters says he felt that he had nothing much to lose: either way, the girl was going to ruin him and so he settled for the least painful of the two. Amery Walters was the last to see her alive. The Sutherlands' godson, John Carrington-Jones, found her drowned next morning out by Beacon Point. Walters' lads (his stable-boys and what-have-you), Peter Walters and young John, who is Peter's best friend, were exercising the horses on the beach around four thirty in the morning. John had cantered on a little bit ahead of the others and he spotted her—a body, that is . . . he didn't realise who it was, or even know the person's sex, until he'd dismounted and waded into the water. Lorna was lying face down, half-submerged in the shallows. At first, it looked like suicide, but after John—"

David hesitated. Then, with a small frown: "Lorna was wearing jeans and a red, brushed cotton, zip-fronted wind-cheater over a denim shirt, and when the wind-cheater was unzipped, up popped another Tarot card. This one, *The Moon*. Then, later on—when the police surgeon took a look at her—marks were found on the back of her neck . . . the kind of markings one would expect to see if someone's, *her*, head had been deliberately held down under water until she'd drowned. There was also a nasty weal on one side of her throat where her initial necklet was ripped from her neck. That hasn't been found, but it was obviously torn from her throat as she struggled with her killer. . . ."

III THE EMPRESS
A Natural Progression

David paused and gazed intently at Mrs. Charles. She was staring past him out of the window. There was no expression on her face, only her eyes, a gradual deepening of their colour, betrayed the intensity of her thoughts.

At length she spoke, her eyes still fixed on some indeterminate object beyond the dainty leaded window-pane.

"A girl," she said abstractedly, "whose clothing gave off a faint but distinct odour of horses and hay, with badly chewed finger-nails and work-roughened hands, and wearing a gold initial necklet . . ."

Abruptly, Mrs. Charles averted her gaze from the window and frowned at David. "But it was an *M* not an *L*."

He stared at her, stunned. "How on earth—?"

"Am I right, Superintendent?"

"Yes, but how—?"

She sighed. "She came to see me the night before I went away. I caught a plane from Heathrow the following day—late in the afternoon of the Fifteenth, the Sunday." She paused and thought for a moment. "Amery Walters was *not* the last person to see Lorna Lock alive. You said he and the girl argued somewhere between eleven and twelve on the Saturday night . . ."

"What time did you see her?" he asked quickly.

"It was shortly after midnight . . ." She paused reflectively. Then, continuing: "The clock in the hall struck the half-hour soon after she arrived. I was thinking about going to bed when there was this dreadful banging on the front door. I naturally assumed that it was someone whose car had broken down or that the driver was lost and he or she was seeking directions."

"Yes, I suppose being so close to the motorway you would get a lot of that."

"Well, no, as a matter of fact, I don't. It's Cyril who usually encounters that sort of thing, his house being that much nearer to the motorway than my bungalow is. But with Cyril away, anyone in trouble would have to continue on along the road towards the village and, of course, I—my bungalow, would be the next place to stop and ask for help. I must confess that I was more inclined to think that it was someone seeking directions because I had heard a car drive up quite normally."

"But Lorna Lock didn't drive," he reminded her. "You're quite sure you heard a car?"

"Positive. I think I mentioned this to you once before . . . This bungalow is set in a slight hollow which acts as a soundshell. Any noise, even a whispered conversation, up on the higher reaches of the access road to the motorway can be heard quite distinctly from inside the bungalow. I didn't see the car she came in . . . it must have been left parked farther down the road and she walked the rest of the way to my front door. But I definitely heard it, Superintendent. Twice . . . Again some minutes after she left."

He frowned thoughtfully. Then, after a moment, he said:

"What did she want with you?"

Mrs. Charles replied hesitantly. "I don't know," she said.

He cocked an eyebrow over the knowing look he gave her and said, "But it was not by chance that she came to *your* front door."

"She came to see Adele Herrmann."

He looked surprised. *"Adele Herrmann!* Why? I mean, how did Lorna Lock know about you and Adele Herrmann, where to find you? She was a London girl."

Again Mrs. Charles hesitated. Then she said, "I have no idea, Superintendent. But whatever or whoever her source of information, she knew that my real name is Adele Herrmann. She also addressed me as *Madame* Herrmann. She did not say who she was."

"Curious," he remarked meditatively. He studied the clairvoyante for a moment. He wasn't sure, but he had a feeling that she was holding out on him, deliberately keeping something back. "Did you know the girl?" he asked, watching her eyes closely.

"No," she replied. "I'd never seen her before, and her name, now that I know it, means nothing to me. I can't remember ever having seen—in my, Adele Herrmann's, professional capacity as a clairvoyante—anyone of that name. Though . . ." She paused and eyed him curiously. "Why did she wear a necklet with the initial *M* if her name was Lorna?"

"That was a bit of a puzzle to start with," he said, "but her sister eventually cleared up that mystery for us . . . the Gidding police. Mrs. Lock—the mother . . . her name was Lorna, too. After she died, Lorna (the daughter) wouldn't have anyone call her by that name and insisted that she should be known by her middle

name, Maude. It's about fifty-fifty. Some people, family
mostly, used *Lorna,* others called her *Maude* or
Maudie."

"I see," said Mrs. Charles, nodding. She was quiet
for a moment or two. Then she gave him a thoughtful
look and said, "The necklet is of some special significance."

"No," he said slowly, puzzled by her tone of voice
which hovered uncertainly somewhere midway between asking a definite question and making a positive
statement of fact. "Only insofar as it's missing. But I
don't think the police are attaching too much im-
portance to it. It obviously came adrift from her neck
and dropped into the sea as she fought for her life,
which means that it could be buried somewhere in the
sand near to where she was found, or that it has drifted
with the tide, perhaps, and is now buried some distance from where the Sutherlands' godson first spotted
her body.

"It was John who noticed that the necklet was
missing. When he reached her, he had no idea how
long she'd been in the water or even if she were dead;
so he dragged her clear of the water on to the beach,
turned her on to her back and undid her wind-cheater,
which was zipped up to her neck—it had a sort of hood
arrangement at the back of it something like an
anorak. Then once he'd loosened all of her restrictive
clothing, he proceeded to give her mouth-to-mouth
resuscitation. But it was too late. She'd gone. Been
dead between two and three hours, the doctor said
later.

"The previous day, while the girl and John were
working about the stables—John spends most of his
time there during the summer holidays—he noticed

that the clasp on the necklet was broken and that the
girl had knotted the ends of the chain together. As
she'd been moving around, the knot had worked its
way from the back of her neck to the front and was
plainly visible alongside the *M*. He told her, in no
uncertain terms, that she was untidy and slovenly—
'a slattern', I believe, were his actual words—and why
didn't she take the necklet to a jeweller and get the
clasp fixed? The incident ended up in quite a slanging
match, and when several of Walters' stable-boys came
running to see what the altercation was about, the
girl—who was screaming at the top of her voice—had
John pinned to a wall with a pitchfork in her hand
and bloody murder, they all swear, on her mind. Then,
when she saw the other lads coming to his rescue, she
turned on them with the pitchfork. They had to grab
it away from her and forcibly restrain her. She got
one of them in the arm. That was the unpleasant incident I referred to a while back, the one that took
place early on the Saturday."

"A nasty experience for the young man concerned."

"It shook everyone up a bit," he said. He smiled
crookedly. "Especially the lad she pitchforked! An
inch or two to the right and she would've speared him
in the chest!"

"The Tarot card left with Lorna Lock . . ." the
clairvoyante began hesitantly. "John, the Sutherlands'
godson, found it?"

"Well, yes and no. By the time he'd got her body
on to the beach, the others had caught him up. Then
for the next few minutes, everyone was too concerned
with his attempts to revive the girl to pay too much
attention to the card when it suddenly appeared inside her wind-cheater. In fact, John unconsciously

tossed it aside. It was after they realised that the girl was dead that one of the other lads took a second look at the card and they started to wonder what it meant, why she'd had it concealed inside her clothing. The police, once they had the pathologist's report and read his conclusions with regard to the marks on the back of her neck, realised that they were more than likely dealing with the Tarot murderer again and that, as before with Miriam Noad, he had left them another clue."

"To what, Superintendent?"

He gave her an odd look. "Well, speaking from my own experience of similar cases, I would say a clue to his identity. He is baiting the police, challenging them to unmask him."

He expected the clairvoyante to agree with him, but she made no comment.

"You disagree?" he enquired after a moment.

"I would hesitate to make a pronouncement of any kind concerning the Tarot murderer's motives, Superintendent. I have not had your experience with murderers."

"But you *know* people," he said, puzzled by her attitude. "You understand the psychology of their thinking . . . what makes one man behave one way and another in a completely different fashion altogether."

She smiled a little. "You flatter me, Superintendent. But . . ." She paused. Then, narrowing her eyes: "You haven't really explained why you have told me all of this . . . why, in what way, you—the Sutherlands—seek my help."

"The Tarot . . . The Sutherlands—*I*—feel that the cards left by the Tarot murderer with his victims are the key to his identity. And, quite frankly, none of us is satisfied with the official findings in that quarter. We would all feel much happier if you would tell us what *you* think the two Tarot cards—*The Star* and *The Moon*—mean. The so-called expert the police have called in to assist them . . . advise on the meanings of the cards—well, he's so puffed up with his own self-importance that as far as I'm concerned, his opinion isn't worth a cracker. You've never heard so much utter nonsense! I could make neither head nor tail of any of it. And if the truth's to be known, no one else can, either. He's one of these eloquent, pseudo-intellectual types who so dazzle you with their brilliance that you instinctively shrink back from questioning their findings too closely for fear of showing your ignorance."

"You are too harsh, Superintendent. Your expert cannot reveal the identity of the Tarot murderer if it isn't there in the cards to be revealed. Not even *I* can do that," she said with a small, mischievous smile.

"Somehow—" He hesitated. Then, frowning and a trifle piqued: "Somehow I get the impression that you don't seem particularly interested in the cards."

She wagged her head reproachfully. "You expect too much too soon, Superintendent. You will have to leave the matter with me for a while—"

"But surely the cards mean *something* to you?" he interrupted her protestingly.

"Oh yes, of course they mean something to me: they reveal quite a lot—"

Sensing that David was again about to interrupt, the clairvoyante held up a hand and said, "No, Superintendent. You must be patient. I need time to think. There are one or two aspects of these crimes which I find highly disturbing and which are going to need a very great deal of careful thought and consideration before I come to any definite conclusions with respect to the Tarot cards which you have mentioned. I would like to ask you three questions and then you must leave me to cogitate."

He looked disappointed but nevertheless nodded his agreement with her wishes. "I can tell the Sutherlands that you will help them?"

"I will give them my interpretation of the significance of the Tarot card which their godson found on Lorna Lock's body: I can promise no more than that."

"Well," he sighed. "That'll be something if not everything that Mary wants. I'm sure she'll be greatly comforted to know that you're willing to take an interest in the matter. She's particularly upset about it."

"That was my first question, Superintendent. Is there some special reason for this concern that the Sutherlands are feeling for their godson? I better than most appreciate that it is never nice to be associated, however slightly, with murder; but it would seem that the Sutherlands are perhaps a little more distressed than one would expect in the circumstances. Surely no guilt has attached itself to their godson over Lorna Lock's death?"

"Not as far as the police are concerned," he replied. "But you know from your own experience of this sort of thing what gossip is," he added ruefully. "How crucifying it can be." He paused, then with an expressive shrug: "John's squabble with the girl—the well-publicised incident with the pitchfork on the Saturday . . . He too attends the same university—He was going to be a veterinary surgeon specialising in horses, thoroughbred racing stock."

"Was?"

"Finding the girl dead, and then all the gossip that's been buzzing around, has apparently shaken him up a bit. He's talking of throwing everything in and not returning to university next term. The Walters boy is of the same mind. James told me that the two of them are now seriously considering joining some half-baked archaeological expedition and spending the next eighteen months digging up the Sahara Desert. The Sutherlands, by the way, are more or less responsible for John while his parents are abroad—his father's a diplomat of some kind or other. His mother was a Gidding girl and she and Mary grew up together. So the ties between Mary and the boy are pretty strong, especially as the Sutherlands never had a family of their own."

He paused. Then, reflectively:

"The way I see it, John and Peter are both suffering from an acute attack of guilty conscience. And not just them. Everyone's suffering from it—John, Peter, the stableboys who gave the girl such a rough time of it . . . they've all elected to overlook the fact that they were merely giving back as good as she gave them. It's even touched the Sutherlands."

"Are you suggesting that that's really why they

would like to see the matter resolved as quickly as possible?"

He nodded. "They don't realise it, of course . . . know what their real motives are. And there's no getting away from the fact that, objectionable and all as she was, Lorna Lock was given a pretty hard time of it by everyone. Nobody, it seems, bothered to take the trouble to find out why, what made her the way she was."

"That, sometimes, is easier said than done," observed Mrs. Charles. "Especially when one is confronted with someone who is as hell-bent on self-destruction as this girl would appear to have been."

He agreed. Then, curiously, he asked, "That was the impression you formed of the girl—assuming, of course, that while there would seem to be very little doubt that we are speaking of the same person, it was indeed Lorna Lock who came here that night? She struck you as being the neurotic, self-destructive sort?"

The clairvoyante hesitated momentarily before replying.

"She had an extremely guilty conscience about something, Superintendent. Curious, isn't it," she remarked thoughtfully, "that both she and everyone associated with her should be similarly troubled?"

"Do you have any idea at all was was bothering her?"

"She spoke to me on my front door-step for barely five minutes. It would take much longer than that to get at the root cause of her guilt. Besides, she refused to be helped."

"Then why bother coming to you in the first place?"

"There is a pattern with these things, Superintendent, and Lorna Lock behaved accordingly, as I would expect of someone in her extreme state of mental agitation. In time—" The clairvoyante broke off and sighed. "But there's never time with the Lorna Locks of this world. They want help and they don't want help, and their confused thinking, this agonising mental conflict, is the beginning of the neurosis, the demon within them which drives them towards their own destruction."

"I remember hearing of a case once, a very long time ago when I first joined the police force," he said meditatively. "It concerned a young man, not unlike Lorna Lock in temperament, who was equally determined on self-annihilation, but either lacked the courage to end it all himself or felt that it was insufficient punishment for whatever sins he imagined he'd committed, and so he systematically set about selecting an executioner, someone to do the job for him. He managed it, too . . . actually talked some pathetically half-witted creature into committing murder. At the trial, the defence claimed that the poor devil had been hypnotised . . . got him off."

He lapsed into a moody, retrospective silence, then, abruptly, he widened his eyes at Mrs. Charles and said, "One wonders if there wasn't something of a similar kind here, but then what of the Tarot murderer's first victim, Miriam Noad . . . a healthy-minded girl who loved life?" He shook his head slowly, sighing. "Three questions, you said?" he reminded the clairvoyante after a small pause.

She nodded. "The next concerns the Tarot cards which were left with the two victims. How were they found?"

He gave her a questioning look.

"Face up, face down?" she queried. "Inverted . . .

that is to say, upside-down—the top of the card towards
the victim's head, or was it the correct way round so
that either girl, had she been able to raise her head
to see the card on her chest, would be looking at it the
way she would were it on a table before her?"

"Face up," he replied. "I know that much. But I'm
not sure about the rest of it. I'll try and find out for
you. It's important, is it?"

"Very much so, Superintendent."

"Yes, I remember now," he said slowly. "You explained it to me once before. It can alter the meaning
of a card, can't it?"

"In some instances, quite dramatically."

A look of concern crossed his face. "We might be
unlucky with the card left on Lorna Lock's body. John
touched it—tossed it aside, remember, before having a
go at trying to bring her round. And I'm not sure if
the police have been made fully aware of the significance of the exact placing of the cards on the girls'
bodies."

"It's of no real consequence in Lorna Lock's case."
The clairvoyante paused and gave him a small, secre-
tive smile. "I know exactly which way round the card
was in that instance."

He stared at her. "How could you possibly know
something like that, Madame?"

He didn't quite catch her murmured reply, but
what he thought he heard her say was, "*Justice* preceding *The Moon*, upright."

David Sayer climbed into his car and sat there staring
thoughtfully at the road ahead. The Sutherlands
would be waiting anxiously for him to report back to
them, but he felt strangely reluctant to leave. There

was something here that he didn't understand, something totally unexpected. He had called on Mrs. Charles, for no other reason, really, than to ask for her interpretation of two symbolic picture cards from the Tarot, and was leaving not with the answers he had hoped to get, or indeed with any answer at all, but with the distinct impression that somehow (and not simply by her admission that Lorna Lock had called on her an hour or two before the girl had been murdered), and with just a few simple, well-chosen questions, Mrs. Charles now knew more about the Tarot murders than the police, or he, did. He was not for one moment suggesting that she was involved in the crimes, but he was now more than ever certain that she was deliberately keeping something back from him relating to them.

Her third question, for example . . . the odd look in her eyes when he had told her that Rupert Roxeth was the Tarot expert who had been called in by the Gidding police to assist them with their enquiries into the Tarot murders. She had denied knowing him personally and had said that she knew him solely by reputation, principally as the author of a number of books on the history of the Tarot.

David frowned. Mrs. Charles had not commented on Roxeth's qualifications, and yet he had garnered the impression that she too regarded them to be somewhat lacking.

A door closed and he looked round quickly. Mrs. Charles had left the bungalow and was coming down the path—towards him, he thought. Then, abruptly, she turned left, away from his car, and walked quickly along the road towards the motorway.

He leaned out of the window and called to her. "Can I give you a lift somewhere?"

"Oh!" she exclaimed. She paused and turned to face him. "I didn't see you there, Superintendent. You gave me quite a start. No, thank you all the same. I'm only going as far as my brother's house, and the exercise will do me good. It's a lovely evening for a stroll, isn't it?"

He agreed and once more they exchanged good nights.

Ten minutes later, he motored slowly past Cyril Forbes' creaky-looking detached house, his gaze picking its way through the maze of wires staying the tall wireless aerial in the front garden to the patch of light which was shining on the tiny attic window, the room in which the clairvoyante's eccentric brother kept the powerful telescope he used to scan the heavens for signs of another visit to Earth by his 'friend' from outer space. Somehow David didn't think that Mrs. Charles would be up there in the attic deputising for her brother. There was, he thought wryly, only one truly loopy person in that family!

Mrs. Charles knelt before the battered tin trunk and then raised the lid. If—and it was a small *if*—she had kept the letter it would be in one of the three big envelopes that she could see wedged tightly between some old books at one end of the trunk. She grunted a little as she prised the envelopes free. Most of the correspondence, she recalled, was destroyed when she finally closed down the Oxford Street premises and moved from London to the country to keep an eye on Cyril. There had seemed little point then in hanging

on to all those old papers, especially any correspondence concerning Lord and Lady Camberley, though
the letter she particularly wanted to read again had,
she seemed to remember, met a fiery fate some little
while before she had left London.

She spent almost an hour sifting through the few
letters which remained from her years as a full-time
practising clairvoyante before giving up all hope of
finding the one that she was seeking. It was as she had
thought. The letter had been burnt soon after she had
read of Lady Camberley's tragic suicide.

Sighing, Mrs. Charles closed the trunk and got to
her feet. There was an old, painted wicker-chair near
the window and she sat down in it. She closed her eyes
and thought back to the time when The Hon. Sophia
Jenkins had consulted her about the future. The
pretty, twenty-one-year-old socialite had received a pro-
posal of marriage from the middle-aged, twice divorced
Lord Camberley, and Sophia—a sincere, serious-minded
young woman—had been unsure of the wisdom of such
a match even though it was an alliance which would
save her impoverished family from some extremely
serious financial embarrassments. She had approached
Madame Herrmann for a reading of the Tarot on the
advice of a mutual friend who had chanced to mention the clairvoyante's name at a fashionable Mayfair
dinner-party.

Sophia, Mrs. Charles recalled, had consulted her in
person only the once. A tiny frown disturbed the
clairvoyante's otherwise perfectly serene brow. Such a
beautiful child, she remembered, and all that tragedy
awaiting her. She had warned Sophia, advised her in
the strongest possible terms not to proceed with the
marriage. And then the threatening letter . . . No, it

was not unfair to call it that. It had definitely contained a threat to her if she failed to heed the writer's warning and continued to advise Sophia against marrying Lord Camberley.

Her eyes still closed, Mrs. Charles rested an elbow on the arm of the chair and stroked her brow pensively. Yes, she could see it now . . . the arrogant handwriting, the boldly dotted *i's* and crossed *t's*, the ambiguous, pretentious signature, *Tarot*.

From the contents of the letter, it had been obvious that *Tarot* was someone very close to Sophia—a member of her immediate family, Mrs. Charles had been inclined to think after reading it . . . someone who desperately, no doubt for financial reasons, wanted the proposed marriage to go ahead—and that that person had a high opinion of himself (Mrs. Charles had been quite certain in her own mind that *Tarot* was a man), and his ability to interpret the meanings of the Tarot cards. However, many years were to pass before Mrs. Charles was to have her suspicions confirmed, and then it was only by chance . . . a letter to the Editor of a London daily newspaper from one Rupert Roxeth on the long-standing controversy concerning the origins of the Tarot. There had been a series of letters on the topic published in the newspaper over a number of days, and Rupert Roxeth's was the last to appear—the final word, so to speak. The Editor, in a short note under Rupert Roxeth's letter, had closed the correspondence on the subject and had then gone on to list the Egyptologist's (Rupert Roxeth was formerly a university professor) academic achievements and qualifications, amongst which credit was given to Professor Roxeth for having been the author of a series of newspaper and magazine articles on the

origins of the Tarot which he had written under the
pseudonym of *Tarot*. A few discreet enquiries on Mrs.
Charles' part had then revealed that Rupert Roxeth
was The (former) Hon. Sophia Jenkins' brother-in-
law.

Mrs. Charles switched her thoughts to Lord Camberley. An unpleasant, widely disliked man and an
exceedingly rich one who cared more for his string
of valuable racehorses and his priceless collection of
jade *objet d'art* than he did for anything or anyone
else, including his beautiful young wife, Sophia. Lord
Camberly's iniquitous behaviour towards her had
driven her to despair. Less than two years after their
marriage, she had begged him for a divorce (Mrs.
Charles had received a most distressing letter from
Lady Camberley at the time), and then when he had
refused to give her one, she had taken an overdose of
veronal and killed herself.

But all of this was a long while in the past, some
fifteen or so years ago. The heirless Lord Camberley,
who had been considerably older than Sophia, had
since died. But Rupert Roxeth was still alive. Very
much so it would seem. And not only had the Gidding
police turned to him for advice, Lorna Lock had also
sought his help. It was too much of a coincidence . . .
The 'Professor Tarot' the girl had spoken of—the
person to whom she had gone with the Tarot card she
had referred to that night, *Justice*—had to be Rupert
Roxeth. And that, thought Mrs. Charles, was very interesting, very interesting indeed. The police, she felt
sure, knew nothing of this. But forgetting that for the
moment, why should Rupert Roxeth, a man who so
vehemently disagreed with Adele Herrmann on interpretation and in almost every other respect con-

cerning the Tarot, purposely open the door for Lorna Lock to come to her and yet warn the girl against listening to any advice that she might have been given? It had to be Rupert Roxeth *(Tarot)* who had told the girl about Adele Herrmann. But that didn't make any sense at all. What were his motives?

A slight chill went through Mrs. Charles. There was something very wrong here, something decidedly unpleasant, and she wished that her brother were there so that she could discuss the matter with him. Cyril, she sighed to herself as she rose to her feet, could be remarkably lucid at times.

Frowning, Mrs. Charles switched out the light and went downstairs.

V   THE POPE
An Approach Is Made

Mrs. Charles was studying the timetable for the morning bus-service between Gidding and Hetley Vale when the telephone rang.

Thelma Braithwaite, Amery Walters' secretary, with admirable economy in the usage of words, briskly explained who she was and the purpose of her call. Feeling a little as though struck by a whirlwind, Mrs. Charles suggested eleven thirty as a suitable time for Miss Braithwaite's employer to call upon her that morning and then replaced the receiver.

Very thoughtfully, she returned to the kitchen and resumed her breakfast. Pouring herself a second cup of coffee, she then picked up the bus timetable and concentrated on the afternoon service to Hetley Vale.

Amery Walters arrived promptly at eleven thirty. Now in his mid-fifties, he had had a short but extremely successful career as a steeplechase jockey before turning to racehorse training for a living and was, as one would imagine, a very small man of excessively neat appearance. On the little finger of his left hand he wore a large diamond ring, and there was another, smaller diamond pinned on his tie.

He sat across from Mrs. Charles in her sitting-room with a closed expression on his face. She was, he observed (as he had been led to expect), an extremely handsome woman . . . a few years younger than himself, he would have thought. There was a little too much jewellery on her fingers to be in what he would call 'good taste', but then the woman had to be an eccentric. . . .

He raised his eyes from the clairvoyante's hands to her face and involuntarily felt himself shrink back from her steady gaze. Eccentric or not, he thought uneasily, there wouldn't be much you could hide from that one. This woman was nobody's fool.

"It was good of you, Madame," he said quickly, crossing his right leg primly over the left, "to agree to see me at such short notice. I am most obliged to you, *most* obliged . . . especially as I've heard it said that you are retired and no longer give consultations—"

"That is not entirely correct, Mr. Walters," she interrupted him quietly. "I have a number of clients who consult me quite regularly: it is simply that with the advancing of the years, I have found it necessary to restrict my list, cut back on my work-load in effect." She paused and smiled. "Mine is a particularly demanding profession and I have always felt honour bound to give of my best, something that one can never do if one allows one's self to become overstretched."

"Does that mean that I have no chance . . . no chance at all," he repeated himself, as was his habit, "of prevailing upon you to accept me as a client?" His look of dismay was rather studied and lacked conviction, but his tone of voice seemed genuine enough. "I should be most disappointed, most disappointed indeed, Madame, if you were to refuse me."

"May I ask who referred you to me?"

"Yes, indeed you may, Madame. It was James Sutherland, the Gidding veterinary surgeon, who prompted me to wonder if you might be able to help me. I believe you and Mr. Sutherland are acquainted. He speaks most highly of you, most highly indeed."

"That is very kind of Mr. Sutherland," murmured Mrs. Charles. She gazed at Amery Walters with frank interest. "In what way was it, Mr. Walters," she said after a moment, "that you anticipated that I should be able to help you?"

"I was given to understand by Mr. Sutherland that you were instrumental in the solving of an old murder which had been committed hereabouts some years ago; and it is in this connection that I seek your help and advice." He leaned forward in his chair and gazed at her intently. "I implore you, Madame, to perform the self-same service for me and unmask the Tarot murderer before this whole ghastly business ruins me."

Mrs. Charles' eyebrows rose. "Ruins you . . . In what way, Mr. Walters?"

"You are familiar with the Tarot murders?" he enquired, eyes narrowed.

"I know something of them, yes," she replied. "I am aware, for instance, that Lorna Lock—the Tarot murderer's second victim—was employed by you as a stable-hand."

He frowned, then nervously uncrossed his legs and squirmed a little in his chair. "A dreadful mistake," he said. "The owners are not happy, not happy at all, about the situation. Strangers—the police—all over the place asking questions, disrupting the routine, upsetting the stable-boys and the horses. Thoroughbred horses are very highly strung creatures, Madame," he said archly. "Extremely temperamental . . . yes, very temperamental indeed. They become tense and neurotic. And that is not the stuff of which champions are made!"

It would be more to the point, thought Mrs. Charles, to say that Amery Walters and Amery Walters alone objected to the strangers and their disruptive influence on his stables.

He himself went on to say more or less much the same thing.

"Some of the owners are most displeased, most displeased indeed. Therefore, Madame, the sooner this whole unfortunate affair is cleared up and forgotten, the happier I shall be. Do I make myself clear?"

"Perfectly," she responded.

"Well, then . . ." he said. "You'll take on the case?"

"No, Mr. Walters, that I'm afraid I cannot do. I think Mr. Sutherland has somewhat misled you . . . quite unintentionally, I'm sure. It is the help of a private detective that you really seek, not that of a clairvoyant. And in any event, I have already agreed to act in my professional capacity as a clairvoyante for another party interested in the Tarot murders which would therefore make it a breach of professional etiquette were I agree to accept you, a second party, as a client on the same matter."

The deep, irregular grooves fanning out across Amery Walters' temples from the corners of his dark eyes contracted into a series of short, sharply defined lines. "I don't suppose you'd be prepared to tell me the name of your client, Madame," he said, a faintly corruptive look in his eye.

She gave him a grave smile. "That too would constitute a breach of professional etiquette, Mr. Walters."

"I see," he said thoughtfully. He studied her for a moment. Then, inclining his head a fraction to one side: "Surely it isn't really possible for someone like you, a clairvoyante, to divine the identity of the Tarot murderer?" He frowned a little. "You did say that you'd been consulted in your professional capacity as a clairvoyante?"

"Only to provide my client with my interpretation of the meanings of the Tarot cards which are connected with the murders," she explained.

"But Roxeth has already done that!"

Something about Amery Walters' tone suggested that Rupert Roxeth was more to him than just a name that he had heard mentioned in connection with the Tarot murders or read in the newspapers.

"Professor Roxeth is a friend of yours?" she enquired.

"Professor?" He looked puzzled. Then his expression cleared and he waved an airy, dismissive hand in the air. "Oh yes . . . Cambridge, wasn't it? Or was it Oxford? Haven't heard him called that—*Professor*—in an age." He paused and eyed her speculatively. "Bit of a scandal there, I seem to remember." His slow, unpleasant smile revealed a row of surprisingly discoloured, badly misshapen teeth. "The usual thing . . . some girl student or other, I believe. Bad influence on young people, they said." A slight narrowing of his eyes accentuated the malicious glint in them. "Got himself kicked out."

The clairvoyante's lack of response to these disclosures seemed to annoy Amery Walters. An angry, embarrassed look swept across his face, and then he remembered that he had not answered her question. "Yes, yes," he said irritably. "I train two horses for him."

The blue eyes widened a little. "I wasn't aware that the Professor was a racing man."

Amery Walters shrugged. "He's not, really: at least,

not in my estimation. He likes to think he is, but he's only an imitation of Camberley—a sorry one at that. Camberley *knew* horses . . . yes, he knew them all right."

"*Lord* Camberley?"

He nodded, wondering a little at the odd expression on the clairvoyante's face. "I used to ride for Camberley . . . before I started up as a trainer. Good many years ago now, of course," he said with a small, fussy frown. "A lot of people didn't like the man—he passed on, you know, quite some while back—but I always found him a very decent sort of chap . . . yes, very decent indeed. I certainly had no complaints about the way he treated me . . . no, no complaints at all."

"I used to know Lady Camberley," she said.

"Ah, yes . . . the beautiful, tragic Sophia," sighed Amery Walters. He shook his head sadly. "A tragedy . . . yes, a real tragedy. Fine horse-woman. A delight to watch." He sighed again at the memory.

"Yes," agreed Mrs. Charles. Her gaze lingered momentarily on Amery Walters, then passed on to some remote object beyond the window. "In that respect she always reminded me very much of my mother."

The clairvoyante shifted her gaze fractionally so that it rested again on her visitor. "My mother was a member of the Italian aristocracy and was also, as is so often the case with ladies of a high-birth, an excellent horse-woman."

She gave a sigh: then with a solemn smile, she continued, "I regret to say that while I am particularly fond of animals, I have never quite conquered my fear of horses. It was a great disappointment for my mother. She took me once on holiday with her to the

Scottish estate of one of her friends, Sir Benedict
Loudoni . . . you have possibly heard of him: he's not
alive now, of course, but in his time, his name was as
well-known in racing circles as Lord Camberley's used
to be. Sir Benedict shared my mother's passion for
horses and riding and they were both most patient and
persevering with me, but I'm afraid that while I had
an exceptional rapport with Jenny, the old donkey on
Sir Benedict's farm, I was frozen stiff with terror at
the mere sight of a horse."

Her smile took on a wistful quality. "I have always
promised myself that I would do something about it.
You know what they say . . . if there's something you
fear, then the best way to conquer that fear is to do
something positive about it—force yourself to do that
thing which frightens you."

The clairvoyant sighed and then looked away. "I
feel that I am a little too old and stiff in the joints
to learn to ride now, but I should like to approach
a horse without my knees turning to jelly and my
mouth drying up.

"But Madame," said Amery Walters. He leant forward and frowned intently at her. "I appreciate and
understand why you cannot help me, but there is
absolutely no reason, no reason at all, why I shouldn't
help you. I insist . . . yes, I simply *insist* that you
should visit my stables and rid yourself of this quite
unnecessary fear. No, no," he said quickly, holding up
his hands as he saw the look of protest come into her
eyes. "*I insist*. Tomorrow afternoon? You have a car?
No? Well, no matter. I shall drive over personally and
collect you. Yes, I shall tell my wife that we will be
entertaining the famous clairvoyante, Madame Adele
Herrmann, to afternoon tea. Lillian will be delighted,

absolutely delighted to meet you. Fancies that she herself has something of a gift for fortune-telling . . . not
with the Tarot, of course. No, not with the Tarot," he
repeated himself, frowning and shaking his head. 'Tea-
leaves. That's Lillian's forte. Or so she likes to think.
Never once hit the nail on the head. If you follow my
meaning, Madame. . . ."

The long bus journey from Gidding to Hetley Vale
gave Mrs. Charles ample time to think over Amery
Walters' visit to her bungalow that morning.

In some ways, he reminded her of the kind of
animal that he trained . . . a pampered, highly strung,
temperamental racehorse. But without the fine breed-
ing. Amery Walters dressed like a gentleman and, for
the most part, spoke and behaved like a gentleman,
but it was very much an acquired pose, deliberately
cultivated. He had not always been a gentleman.
There was a shrewdness, an animal cunning, in his
dark brown eyes that Mrs. Charles instinctively dis-
trusted. Amery Walters was a man who had clawed
his way into his present position, a man who would
cling on to his gains like grim death, selfishly so. His
invitation to visit his stables had been a little too
quick. Racehorse trainers, those whom Mrs. Charles
had known in the past, did not welcome sightseers to
their stables, not unless there was something in it for
them . . . the possibility of some business, a horse that
they hoped to be invited to train.

No, it had all been far too easy. What she had hoped
for, yes . . . But why so insistent? she asked herself.
The logical answer was that he hoped to persuade her
to change her mind about helping him, but that didn't
fit his character. He wasn't a man to waste his time

on lost causes, or to have difficulty recognising one
when he saw it: in that way, his selfishness was as
studied as everything else about him. But, she reflected, he had been noticeably thoughtful after she
had told him that she had already been approached
about the Tarot murders. Was that his motive for
insisting on her visit? To so disarm her that she would
disclose the name of her client? Or did he want her
there at the stables, where Lorna Lock had worked,
for some other, more personal reason? It wasn't her
impression that Amery Walters knew that James Sutherland, through the good offices of a friend, had
sought help from the clairvoyante he had recom-
mended to him. It could, of course, have been quite
some while ago that James Sutherland had spoken of
her to Amery Walters. Then again, she could be wrong
and Amery Walters might know very well that she
was interested in the Tarot murders on the Sutherlands' behalf.

Something that David Sayer had said to her the
previous evening suddenly flashed through her mind.
Could it be, she wondered, that we have another case
of an acutely guilty conscience? Amery Walters hadn't
shown any more kindness to the girl than anyone else
had. And one mustn't lose sight of Peter Walters in
all of this, she reminded herself. His father hadn't
once mentioned his name. Where was the fatherly
concern, the concern that any normal, caring parent
would have over a son who was a known antagonist of
a murder victim? Was Amery Walters really only worried about himself?

She sighed. She had come the full circle and was
right back where she had started. . . .

VI   THE LOVERS
A Possible Dilemma of Choice

Mrs. Charles arrived at No. 3 Amberley Drive, a small, unpretentious semi-detached house not far from the centre of Hetley Vale, shortly after two in the afternoon. She had not telephoned beforehand: people were seldom favourably disposed towards discussing a bereavement, especially a tragic one, with strangers; and while a preliminary telephone call would have been the correct, courteous approach to the late Miriam Noad's family, it could have resulted in a refusal to discuss the girl's death, a risk that Mrs. Charles was particularly anxious to avoid.

The door was opened by a middle-aged woman who, judging by her ill-fitting clothing, had lost a considerable amount of weight over a short, fairly recent period. She also looked tired, as if she had not had a good night's rest in a very long while.

Mrs. Charles spoke first. "Mrs. Noad?" she enquired.

The woman nodded listlessly. Someone else selling clothes or cosmetic from a catalogue, she thought wearily. Why didn't they leave her alone? She started to close the door.

Mrs. Charles moved a little nearer. "Good afternoon," she said in a firm, clear voice. "I am Adele Herrmann. Madame Herrmann. You may have heard of me."

Mrs. Noad eyed her up and down. "No," she said disinterestedly. "I'm sorry, but you'll have to excuse me. I'm not well. I must lie down. I can't see anyone today."

The gap between the door and the jamb narrowed resolutely to within fractions of an inch of the point where the door would click shut and then there was a hesitant pause. Mrs. Charles held her breath and waited. The seconds ticked by. Then, very slowly, the door reopened and Mrs. Noad stared at her.

"That murder . . . The one in the small village not far from Gidding." Mrs. Noad spoke hesitantly, her fixed gaze boring mercilessly into her visitor. "You're the clairvoyante . . . the one they thought did it, aren't you? I read about it in the papers. You found out who really murdered that old woman, didn't you?"

Mrs. Charles privately thanked heaven for the natural curiosity of the normal, average person where murder and crimes of violence were concerned. She smiled gravely. "Not entirely on my own. I did have some help . . . A friend of mine, a retired chief superintendent of police, must be given his share of the credit for solving that murder. Without his expert assistance, the real murderer might never have been apprehended."

"Is he—this policeman friend of yours—why you're here? To—" Mrs. Noad's bottom lip quivered. Her voice was tremulous. "To find out who murdered my beautiful little girl?"

Mrs. Charles regarded her kindly. "I wonder if I might come in, Mrs. Noad?" she enquired gently. "Just for a few moments. . . ."

Mrs. Noad nodded and fumbled round the belt of her cotton-print dress for the handkerchief which she kept tucked there.

They went through to the living-room and sat down.

Mrs. Noad dabbed at her eyes with the handkerchief. "Her father and I will never understand it," she said thickly. "*Never!* Miriam was such a *sensible* girl. She'd never have accepted a lift from a stranger. She was a good girl, not cheap like some people round here are saying." She covered her face with the handkerchief and cried bitterly into it. "They didn't know her: they've got no right to talk like that about her. It's not true. She *was* a good girl," she wept. "Miriam wasn't interested in men, boy friends. First things first, she always said. Her nursing— That's all she ever really cared about. She was a good girl."

"I know, I know," said Mrs. Charles soothingly.

Mrs. Noad stopped weeping and gave her a teary look. "How?" she asked dolorously. "How would you know?"

"*The Star*, Mrs. Noad . . . the Tarot card that was found with your daughter: that's how I know that Miriam was everything you believed her to be. And the person who murdered her knew it, too. That was why he chose that card."

"But . . . " Mrs. Noad frowned hard at the clairvoyante. Then with a loud sniff: "The police, the newspapers . . . that man—the expert who's helping the police: he said that the Tarot card was left by Miriam's killer as a clue to his identity. They all said that it was the Tarot murderer's way of challenging everyone to find out who he was."

The clairvoyante was shaking her head. "No, Mrs. Noad," she said firmly. "The Tarot card which was left with your daughter was a clue to *her* identity. It embodied *her* character and personality, not the Tarot murderer's. The police, I regret to say, have been completely misled: they have been looking at that clue the wrong way round."

The other woman looked bewildered. "You mean it's not as important as they think?"

"It's important, *very* important, but not in the way that they have been led to believe. And in any event, *The Star* was only half a clue. There was another Tarot card."

"Another card?" Mrs. Noad's eyes were very big and round. "Nobody told us anything about another card. Why haven't the police said something to us?"

"For the very simple reason, Mrs. Noad, that they know nothing about it." The clairvoyante hesitated. Then choosing her words carefully, she went on: "And I should like to stress that this is only an opinion, a strongly held belief of mine that there was another Tarot card involved in your daughter's murder . . . one which she would have received some time prior to her death—a day, several days, perhaps, before she was murdered."

Mrs. Noad was frowning and shaking her head. "Miriam never received anything like that. I'm sure of it. She would've said something."

"You're quite sure about that . . . that your daughter would've mentioned something of that nature to you?"

Mrs. Noad's frown deepened. "Yes," she said hesitantly. "I *think* so."

"Nothing came for her in the mail which she subsequently refused, or seemed reluctant, to discuss with you?"

Mrs. Noad shook her head slowly. "Miriam didn't receive any post at all before—" She faltered, her bottom lip trembling. Then she swallowed quickly and went on: "She only got home the day before . . . before it happened—on the Friday."

"Your daughter had come home for the weekend?"

"Mrs. Noad frowned a little. "To tell the truth, I'm not really sure. I don't think Miriam knew, either. She'd not been very well, you see, and the hospital . . . you know, where she was doing her training . . . they say she had to have a rest. If she didn't go easy for a bit . . . well, they seemed to think she was heading for a nervous breakdown. She was always a very studious girl . . . serious, hardworking. She was just over-tired, I think . . . been working and studying too hard and needed a break. A few days' rest and she would've been her old self again." Her voice caught and she lowered her eyes to the handkerchief which she was tugging and twisting nervously between her fingers.

"You had noticed a change in your daughter, Mrs. Noad?"

Mrs. Noad dabbed at her eyes and sniffed. "Her father was so proud of her, but . . ." She paused, frowning at the handkerchief before putting it to her eyes again. "He pushed— I *warned* him! I saw the signs last Christmas. Miriam was trying too hard. She was always top of her class, you see—even when she was a little girl . . . always got the highest marks and the best report in the class. 'What did it matter if she came second or third or fourth?' I used to say to her father. Just so long as she passed . . . that was all that really mattered. But no," she said bitterly. "His little girl had to be the best. It was all right for her in Hetley Vale. You see, here she was a big fish in a little pond. But over there in Gidding . . . It's such a huge place now—much bigger than Hetley Vale—and the competition was far greater."

"There was a problem with her training, her studies?"

"Oh no," said Mrs. Noad quickly. "Not in the way that you're probably thinking. Miriam was still top girl, the best in the class. But the strain was getting to be too much for her. She couldn't keep it up: it wasn't fair to expect it of her."

"Did your daughter discuss her training with you, confess that the pressures of studying and working hard at the hospital were beginning to get on top of her?"

Mrs. Noad shook her head sadly. "Miriam wasn't one for talking about her problems. She sorted things out for herself, right from the moment she first learnt to walk and talk. She was a very independent girl."

"And a very happy one, I've been told," said Mrs. Charles.

"Yes." Mrs. Noad nodded her head quickly and pressed the handkerchief against her eyes. "But the signs were there. There are some things that a mother can always see."

Mrs. Charles regarded her thoughtfully. "You first observed the change in your daughter when she came home last Christmas?"

"Miriam didn't come home for Christmas. She couldn't get off. We—her father and I—went to her: she was on duty Christmas Night, but we spent Christmas Day together in her flat. Most of it, anyway. She had to give a bit of a hand at The Good Samaritan with the Christmas dinners. That was in the morning: so while she was down there, I got busy and popped the turkey in the oven for us . . . had everything ready by the time she got back."

The remembrance made Mrs. Noad start weeping afresh.

"The Good Samaritan," murmured Mrs. Charles. "I've heard that name somewhere . . . other than in the Bible, I mean."

Mrs. Noad wiped her eyes and then blew her nose. "It's one of these . . . well, a *soup kitchen,* I suppose you'd call it. For down-and-outs. Run by St. Luke's . . . the little C. of E. church in Lowland Road. You pass it in the bus from Gidding."

"Yes," said Mrs. Charles, nodding pensively. "I know the one you mean."

"The church leases an old warehouse near the town centre and Miriam and a lot of other young people over in Gidding helped convert it into some kind of halfway house . . . *I think* that's what Miriam called it. No one is preached to or anything like that, but those who want to can stop there—young people on drugs and alcoholics mostly. All very depressing, I've always thought. I would've much preferred Miriam to have done some other form of social work. Perhaps with handicapped children or something like that. Something *nice.* It used to worry me . . . you know, thinking about her working with those people—drug addicts. She'd led a fairly sheltered life and . . . well . . . it just wasn't *nice!*"

Mrs. Noad's nose wrinkled and she drew back her top lip over her teeth in a singularly expressive gesture which could have left no one in any doubt about how distasteful she personally found the form of social work carried out by her late daughter at The Good Samaritan. She went on:

"Even her father was worried when she told him

about it, and that was unusual for him. As a rule,
anything Miriam did or wanted to do was all right
by him. She took on too much, that was the real
trouble. Every time we saw her there would be something else . . . more committees, more fund raising—
she was never still! She had enough on her plate,
especially this year as one of the entrants in the Miss
Gidding General competition. She should *never* have
got involved with The Good Samaritan. I was never
happy about it."

"You felt that this social work was depressing her?"

"Well, it must have got her down, mustn't it? It
would anybody. She started helping them in her free
time somewhere around September last year; and as
I've said, by Christmas, the strain of it all was definitely
beginning to show. She was very nervy. Her father
said he couldn't see it, but I could. A mother can. She
was very tense, on edge all the time. Very controlled
about it, mind you. Miriam was never one for scenes.
But," sighed Mrs. Noad heavily, "it was there, under-
neath the smiles and all the joking. The tension . . .
I could see it. So could Karen, Miriam's flat-mate. I
had a quiet word with her, Karen, before we left on
Christmas Night—you know, without letting on to
Miriam or to my husband—and asked her to keep an
eye on Miriam for me and to let me know if things
got any worse."

"You said your daughter's friend had also observed
a change in her?"

"Yes. Karen was very loyal and wouldn't say much,
but you could tell that they'd been having words . . .
not been getting along too well. And they'd always
been the *very* best of friends. Karen is a secretary at
the hospital . . . that's where they met. A surprising

sort of friendship, really," commented Mrs. Noad, a wistful far away expression in her eyes. "I mean, that Miriam and Karen got on so well together. They weren't a bit alike. I know they say that opposites attract, but Karen is all the things that *I* always thought Miriam despised."

Mrs. Noad paused and gave a deep sigh. "Miriam was a very liberated young woman. She couldn't bear to see women degrading themselves by using their sex to get what they wanted out of life." She raised her eyebrows at Mrs. Charles. "In our day, we—that is, you and I—would've called girls like Karen little gold-diggers. Knows exactly what she wants, does that one. And she'll get it!"

Mrs. Noad's eyes took on another wistful, dreamy look and for the moment, Mrs. Charles left her quietly with her thoughts.

After an appropriate interval, the clairvoyante then pressed on with her quest.

"Did Karen make any comment about your daughter's edginess?" she asked.

"No, not really," Mrs. Noad responded. "She just agreed with me that Miriam had been doing far too much and that she hadn't been getting anywhere near enough rest."

Mrs. Charles' eyebrows rose interrogatively. "Are your daughter's belongings still at the flat she shared with Karen?"

"No," said Mrs. Noad, shaking her head. "I went over there after the police had finished with every-thing. Karen went through her things with me. There wasn't a great deal of stuff to be sorted out: Miriam wasn't one for collecting things . . . liked everything

neat and tidy, just so! Karen helped me to pack everything up. I brought most of it home with me."

The clairvoyante's eyebrows came together in a faint
frown. "You didn't find a Tarot card amongst your
daughter's things?"

Mrs. Noad shook her head and widened her eyes.
"Miriam didn't even own a pack of ordinary playing-
cards." She paused and considered Mrs. Charles very
thoughtfully. "Why is the second Tarot card so important to you?"

"It's not the *second* card that interests me, Mrs.
Noad," explained the clairvoyante quietly. "*The Star*
was the second card. It's the *first* card that really matters now, and I must know what it was, which card
your daughter received from the Tarot murderer prior
to her leaving this house on the night she died."

Mrs. Noad frowned at her. "Would it . . . that first
card—if there really was another one that nobody
knows anything about—tell you who murdered our
girl?"

"It would confirm that I am thinking along the
right lines," replied the clairvoyante carefully.

There was a long pause, then Mrs. Noad said, "You
speak almost as if—" Her voice dropped to a shocked
whisper. "*You know, don't you? It's there in your eyes,
in your voice, in all the questions that you've been
asking me. You can see that it's going to happen
again. . . .*"

VII   THE CHARIOT
Something Unexpected

Amery and Lillian Walters were at pains to be perfect host and hostess.

Mrs. Walters served afternoon tea chattering light-heartedly about the continuing drought and what it had done to her runner beans, and then, more seriously, went on to attack the poor prize-money to be won in British horse-racing as compared with other parts of the world . . . And was Mrs. Charles at all interested in horse-racing?

No mention was made by either Mr. or Mrs. Walters of the tragedy which had occurred recently in their midst and, their visitor observed with interest, Lillian Walters pounced with increasing nervousness on any lull in the conversation, however slight, as if she were playing a game where points were awarded to the person who succeeded in bridging the gap with the greatest possible speed. Clairvoyance, like the Tarot murders, Mrs. Charles also observed with interest, was obviously another subject to be avoided at all costs. Not once did Lillian Walters refer or even hint at the occult talent which her husband had ascribed to her; and that, thought Mrs. Charles, made Lillian Walters quite unique. Amateur fortune-tellers, those of Mrs. Charles' acquaintance, were not usually so reticent about their skills.

At length, Amery Walters and Mrs. Charles rose, and the horse-trainer then escorted his visitor over his stables, which he modestly referred to as 'not as big as some . . . indeed no, not as big as some.' Very quickly, Mrs. Charles formed quite the opposite opinion, that Amery Walters' racing stables were bigger and better equipped than most.

Amery Walters had everything—even, incredulously, an indoor swimming pool for the horses he trained. The pool was still in the course of construction and while Amery Walters was being perfectly serious when he claimed that it was to be used exclusively by his valuable charges, Mrs. Charles could hardly be blamed for wondering if this were not his way of teasing her for having made an earlier remark to him that his stables appeared to lack nothing.

"But surely," she protested, "with the beach and the sea so near at hand, there would be no need for a swimming pool?"

There was a hint of a smile in Amery Walters' eyes, as if he had indeed enjoyed a small joke at his visitor's expense, but then he went on to explain the pool's true purpose.

"It's really intended for horses which have suffered injuries . . . physical therapy for them. They can swim . . . yes, indeed, they can swim, get exercise that way, whereas some forms of injury would not permit of the more strenuous exercise that they normally get on the beach. Here in the swimming pool, we will be able to control and regulate just how much exercise an injured animal gets. And, of course, there's always the added benefit of the mental therapy for the sick horse. He's got something to look forward to and—"

A slim blonde in a buff-coloured raw silk trouser-suit suddenly approached them from around the side of one of the outbuildings and, with a brusque apology for the interruption, told Mr. Walters that there was an urgent phone call for him up at the house.

"One of the owners, I daresay," he sighed to Mrs. Charles. "Yes, one of the owners for sure. Everything is urgent to them. If you'll just whisper a few sweet nothings in the caller's ear for a moment, Miss Braithwaite, I'll be along in a second or two . . . yes, I'll be right there in just a minute."

With a disapproving look on her face, Miss Braithwaite gave a curt nod of her head, then turned and walked smartly back to the house.

"My secretary," Amery Walters explained unnecessarily. He lowered his voice. "Dry as dust. No sense of humour at all . . . no, no sense of humour at all." He raised an arm and hailed one of the stable-hands who happened to be passing.

"If you don't mind, Madame," said Amery Walters abruptly. "Old Jack will finish showing you around. There's not much more to be seen anyway. I'm sorry to abandon you like this, but you know how it is . . . duty calls and all that!"

Mrs. Charles brushed aside his apology with an expression of her gratitude for the time that he had spared her when she know how very busy he must be: then, as Amery Walters hurried after his secretary, Mrs. Charles turned to the small gnome-like man who the trainer had called 'Old Jack'. He was studying her with a peculiar, knowing little smile on his lips.

She raised her eyebrows. "Is something wrong?" she enquired.

"I've been watching you," he confessed. "You and the guv'nor." He cackled throatily. "Phobia, my eye! You ain't never been scared of a horse in your life. Natural affinity, that's what you've got."

She studied him for a moment. "I see I haven't been as clever as I had hoped to be," she observed dryly. "I presume then, as I was so patently transparent in your eyes, that Mr. Walters would've similarly seen through my little deception?"

Old Jack gave a huge, gummy grin. There was a wide gap between his small, sharply pointed canines which were surprisingly white and healthy-looking in view of the absence of the teeth which had once filled the intervening space.

"Mr. Walters ain't normally easily fooled. I reckon as he saw through you. Doesn't like being taken for a fool, neither. Not as a rule. But then, this is different. Got to swallow your pride sometimes . . . you know, when that's all that stands between you and getting what you want."

"And what is it that Mr. Walters wants from me that he is apparently willing to so humble himself?" she enquired coolly.

"*Go on with you!*" he said with another peculiar, all-knowing look. "Anyone can see what's up wi' him. He's got a guilty conscience, hasn't he? He wants somebody to prove that young Lorna was murdered and that she didn't go racing off and commit suicide after the barney he had with her the night she was done in. He hopes that that somebody is going to be you."

She looked surprised. "I thought that suicide had been ruled out—"

"By the police," he interrupted her with a small grin. "Not by Mr. Walters. He's dead scared he pushed her into it. She was as nutty as a fruit-cake, you know," he said, wide-eyed. "Barmy ain't the word for it!'

"But the marks on the back of her neck where, as I was given to understand it, somebody forcibly held her head under water—"

Old Jack gave another gummy grin. "That was me. I was the one what done that to her."

Mrs. Charles eyed him thoughtfully. "You mean you're admitting to having held Lorna Lock's head under water until she drowned?"

"No, no, of course not." The grin vanished and was replaced with an impatient frown. "The bruises on the back of her neck . . . That's what I did to her —when I caught her snooping round the horse-boxes late that night . . . the night she was done away with. Grabbed her by the scruff of the neck, I did . . . frog-marched her all the way up to the house and into the guv'nor's office. The she-devil bit me," he said plaintively, holding out his right forearm and frowning unhappily at a small area of skin where the disposition of a number of tiny white scars did indeed resemble a bite mark. He went on:

"I had to get a good hold on her or else she would've done me a proper mischief. Little tiger she was when she got riled up about something. Kicked and clawed and scratched and bit. The others were bloody terrified of her, but me . . ." The grin suddenly reappeared. "I know how to deal with 'em. Only one way to handle a she-cat. Grab 'em by the scruff of the neck and shake the livin' daylights outa them."

"You don't appear to be suffering your employer's sense of guilt over the incidents of that night," observed Mrs. Charles.

"I was only doing my job, following the guv'nor's instructions," he replied airily. "It was more than my life was worth to have turned a blind eye to her. She had no business being anywhere near the horses at that hour o' night . . . been told a hundred times to clear orf outa there."

"You were on guard duty that night?"

He nodded. "I went on at nine and finished just before twelve when young Peter took over."

"Mr. Walters' son?"

He nodded again, "Peter and Eddie swapped shifts. Eddie's one of the apprentice jockeys, and he and Peter's mate, John, wanted to go into Gidding to one of them newfangled dance halls . . . you know, all noise and advanced St. Vitus' dance . . . none of your actual style like we used to have in my young day." Old Jack laid his right arm across his waist, and with his left arm held aloft, and a dreamy expression on his face, went into an extremely graceful waltz. Finishing with a neat pirouette, he then went on:

"Peter got hurt in that punch up wi' Lorna earlier in the day. Ricked his ankle. So he couldn't go with 'em anyway."

"Punch-up?" Mrs. Charles looked puzzled. "Oh, you mean that incident with the pitchfork?"

"Oooh, but that young lady was mad," said Old Jack, eyes shining. "*Hopping* mad! She'd have done him in if the others hadn't heard her screaming at him."

Mrs. Charles gave him a curious look. "Peter, you mean?"

"No, young Carrington-Jones . . . Peter's mate, John. Peter did in his ankle when he tried to get the pitchfork off her. She sorta swung round and belted him square in the breadbasket and over he went like a ninepin, flat on his back. They say that

people what are off their rocker—barmy—don't know
their own strength. And, by golly, when that girl was
mad, she could fight like a demon. Strong as a man,
she was. Took four of 'em to hold her still once they'd
got the pitchfork away from her."

"I understand that this sort of thing happened
fairly frequently."

"Practically every day . . . Somebody would say the
wrong thing to her—and it didn't take much, I can tell
you—and *pow!*" He curled the short, stubby fingers
on his right hand into a tight fist and slammed it
emphatically into his other hand. "The fireworks
would start, and no mistake about it! That is," he said,
frowning, "up until a couple of days before she was
done in. All of a sudden she calmed right down.
Peculiar it was . . . as if she had something on her
mind and couldn't be bothered wi' anything else but
whatever it was she was thinking about. Then on the
Saturday when John picked on her for looking so
scruffy, orf she went again. Mighta known it was the
calm before the storm," he observed dourly.

"Did any one particular person figure more in these
outbursts of temper of hers than anyone else?"

"Nope. She treated us all alike. With utter contempt.
That little lady was so full of hate and malice it just
wasn't true."

"I don't understand—" Mrs. Charles paused and
frowned. "If there was nothing, no one that she liked,
why was she so insistent that she should come here
to work this summer?"

Old Jack laughed. "Potty about him, wasn't she?
She pretended she wasn't, but I reckon it was pretty
plain to see that she fancied him."

"Who?"

"Young Peter. Mr. Walters' lad. Mucked up that
play of his . . . made a right proper charley of him
in front of everyone. Then she gets that mate of her
ol' man's to twist the guv'nor's arm into letting her
work here for the holidays, and no sooner does she
get here than she starts picking on him—young Peter,
I mean . . . making a proper little nuisance of herself around him all the time. Oh, I know we all
came in for our fair share of trouble from her, but
you'll never convince me she wasn't gone on him.
That's why we had all the aggravation from her . . .
because young Peter paid her no mind and did his
best to keep outa her way. Really made her foam at
the mouth, that did. And like a small kid, she knew
that the only way she could get him to take any notice of her at all was by behaving just like that . . . as
if she was a spoilt brat, and throwing a temper tan-
trum."

"What was she doing near the horse-boxes that
Saturday night?"

A look of caution came into Old Jack's milky-brown
eyes. He shrugged. "Who had time to ask them sorta
questions? I had too much else on me mind . . . like
how to stop her biting a great chunk outa me arm."

"Little Eva—the horse she rode without permission
. . . Lorna was in her horse-box again, was she?"

"No," he said. "It was just one of the horses . . .
nothing special, like Little Eva is." He narrowed his
eyes and stared hard at something in the distance;
but before he could make a reality of the thought
which was uppermost on his mind and change the
subject, Mrs. Charles said:

"But even so, you felt her breach of discipline was

serious enough to warrant drawing Mr. Walters' attention to the matter?"

He looked uncomfortable. "You don't understand— A girl like that . . . malicious . . . you never knew what she'd do next. She could've caused alot of trouble for the guv'nor."

Mrs. Charles considered the elderly stable-boy very thoughtfully. "Are you ever cruel to animals, Jack?" she enquired quietly.

He gave a violent start. "*Me?* No, never!" He glanced about him anxiously. "That sorta talk, lady, could cost a man his job."

"Even when it's not true?'

"I never hurt a horse in my life," he said firmly. "I'm like you . . . Got the affinity. You and I . . . we'd sooner cut orf our right arms than—"

"Than do what, Jack?" asked Mrs. Charles softly.

Old Jack's eyes darted nervously from one corner of the yard to another. "Well, sometimes— This is just between you and me, missus . . ." He tapped the side of his squat nose with a forefinger. "Strictly confidential, you understand. Sometimes you get a horse what has got the ability, but you know, it's thick up top— thicker than most—and somehow you've got to get it through to him what's expected of him."

"I think I understand," she said slowly. "An animal which fails to respond in the desired manner is disciplined not with the customary whip, but with a more primitive—"

"Lady, *please.*" Again Old Jack's eyes darted nervously into each corner of the yard. "It's bad, it's wrong . . . nothing, *no one,* would ever get *me* to do that sort of thing, but sometimes—"

"Sometimes," intoned Mrs. Charles heavily, "a

trainer is obliged to carry out a certain owner's instructions despite his personal revulsion and objection to what has been suggested."

Old Jack looked very frightened. He spoke quickly, barely pausing for breath. "The guv'nor was dead against it. Upset, he was. And young John and the girl when they found out. John's going to be a vet. Mad he is about horses and dogs . . . horses, mostly. And the girl—I'll say this for her: she was crazy about horses. Never lost her temper wi' any of them. Kindness itself. Could ride, too. Handled Little Eva like she was one of them pussy-cat ponies the kids have rides on down at the beach. Ain't too many of us what can claim that about Little Eva. Given me a few scares, I can tell you. She's as temperamental as the girl was . . . bites, too, if you're silly enough to make the mistake of turning your back on her for anything longer than half a second. That's probably why the two of 'em hit if off so well together. They understood one another."

"Lorna was snooping around the horse-boxes that night looking to see if any—" Mrs. Charles broke off and fixed a stern, uncompromising eye on Old Jack. "Or was it the ill-treatment of one particular horse that she was concerned about that night?"

Old Jack nodded miserably and suddenly lost his volubility. The words came out very reluctantly and his sentences were spaced alternately with a heavy sigh and a look of wide-eyed indignation.

"Not a hair of his head had been touched. The guv'nor was sticking to his guns. It was dead against his principles, he said. But, well . . . the Professor said he wasn't going to waste any more of his money and threatened to have the horse butchered for pet food. Never lets anyone get the better of him, does that one," he interpolated sourly. "Do it out of sheer bloody-mindedness, just to show everyone that he meant what he'd said. And then you've got to make up your mind, don't you? Ask yourself what's the lesser of the two evils— A little bit of unpleasantness till the horse gets the message, or the butcher's slab?"

"I see," she said nodding slowly. "The horse in question belongs to Rupert Roxeth."

"One of his. He's got two with the guv'nor. The other one's not much good, neither. Got more brains but it's short on staying power. I dunno why it is," he muttered. "It always seems to me that often as not it's the wrong people what have got all the money."

"And own racehorses?"

Old Jack nodded morosely. "Roxeth should never be let near a hundred miles of an animal, *any* animal. Got a right sadistic streak in him. Loves to see poor dumb creatures get hurt and suffer. He's sick in the head if you ask me."

"Who's that you're talking out of turn about this time, Jack?" a voice behind them enquired coldly.

Mrs. Charles turned towards the voice. A tall, very thin, bespectacled young man in his early twenties was frowning at them.

Old Jack murmured something which the young man irritably brushed aside with what sounded like an oft-repeated warning about discussing owners with visitors to the stables: then he introduced himself to Mrs. Charles.

"Peter Walters," he said abruptly. "Father sent me out with his apologies. I'm afraid that something important has cropped up and he won't be able to drive you back to the village, but I'd be happy to whenever yon're ready to leave."

The young man's tone of voice suggested that in his opinion that time had come.

"Thank you, but no," said Mrs. Charles. "The bus stop is quite handy, I understand: and in any event, I must break my journey and attend to some business in Gidding before making my way back home."

Peter did not argue with her. He scowled a little and turned away.

Mrs. Charles glanced round to bid good-bye to Old Jack but he had disappeared. Looking back at Peter, who was walking quickly away from her, she then remarked, "I see that the Professor has warned you about me, too."

Peter paused. Then, very slowly, he turned and retraced his steps. There was something faintly ar-

rogant and mocking about the tilt of his head and
the way he narrowed his eyes at her as he spoke.

"The Professor—Roxeth, you mean?"

"He was a professor once, wasn't he? An Egyptologist?"

"Yes, I believe so. But not many people call him
that . . . Professor, I mean."

"Do you?"

Peter considered the question. After a moment or
two, he shrugged and said, "Sometimes." He hesitated. Then, very curtly: "I shouldn't take too much
notice of anything Old Jack said, if I were you. He
tends to romanticise."

"About whom? Professor Roxeth? Or are you referring to the bruising that he says he caused on the
back of Lorna Lock's neck?"

Peter laughed lightly. "Oh, he told you that yarn,
did he?"

"It's not true?"

"When I saw the two of them that night, it was
difficult to say who was dragging whom before the lord
and master. As an impartial observer," he said dryly,
"I would've said that Lorna was winning by a good
half-nelson."

"She was taking *him* up to the house to see your
father? It wasn't the other way round?"

"As I've said, it was hard to tell. But in view of
the fact that she'd always got the better of Old Jack
before, I don't see why he should suddenly come up a
winner that night."

"I don't understand," said Mrs. Charles hesitantly.
"Why lie about it?"

"To save face. The lads would've teased the very
devil out of him about it. Like they always did."

"But surely—" Mrs. Charles hesitated, looked puzzled. "The argument your father had with Lorna that night . . . surely that was because she had defied his instructions not to go near the horses?"

"So he said," the young man replied abruptly. There was a small pause. Then, narrowing his eyes, he went on: "Old Jack's been with my father for a very long time . . . they were stable-boys together. My father is one of the old school . . . you know, loyalty to one's old friends and to those who have served you well and faithfully. Regardless."

"Lorna made some complaint to your father about Jack?"

"I didn't hear any of their conversation," he said off-handedly. "I merely wanted to point out to you that there is always an area of doubt where Old Jack is concerned and never more so than with anything that he claims to have said or done. When I saw the two of them—that was right here in the stable-yard as I was on my way to relieve Old Jack—he was definitely getting the worst of it."

"You made no attempt to intercede?"

"I'd made that mistake once before that day," he said very dryly. "I wasn't about to step into the lion's cage again. Certainly not for Old Jack. He was only getting what he asked for. He deliberately antagonised her, usually when there were plenty of other lads about to come to his rescue. It was only a matter of time before she cornered him on his own and gave him a good thumping."

"Did you see her leave that night?"

"No," he said shortly.

She eyed him contemplatively. "Why did your father really come to see me yesterday, Peter?"

"Didn't he tell you?"

Mrs. Charles did not reply.

He stared at her for a moment, then thrust his hands into his trouser-pockets and shrugged indifferently. Smirking unpleasantly, he said, "A little dicky-bird told him that you've been hired to look into Lorna's death and he hoped you'd tell him who that someone is . . . whether one of the owners has sicked you on to him. Judging by the look on his face when he came into the house a few minutes ago, I'd say he didn't get it out of you today, either."

"Why should that aspect of my interest in the Tarot murders be of so much interest to him? I find it difficult to believe that this affair could in any way jeopardise his career as a racehorse trainer, nor does it seem at all likely to me that he would imagine that it could be a threat to him. Wouldn't it be more reasonable to expect that he is concerned about the effect that Lorna Lock's death might have on you?"

"My father concerned about me? That's funny," said Peter with no outward appearance of mirth of any kind. *"Really* funny!" He looked at his watch. "If you're quite sure that I can't drive you at least as far as Gidding, then I woulld suggest that you should make a start now for the bus stop. The service isn't particularly good; and if you miss the next bus, you'll have something like a forty-minute wait."

They crossed the yard and then strolled leisurely towards the barn-like, thatched mock-Tudor house.

"Did you know Miriam Noad, the first Tarot victim?" enquired Mrs. Charles conversationally.

Peter was squinting up at the smoky blue sky. "No," he replied. "She wasn't someone from round here, was she? I know most of the local talent, anything that's worth knowing. . . ."

As they reached the house, he paused and said, "The best of British luck to you!"

A slight movement in the leaded window behind him drew Mrs. Charles' thoughtful gaze away from his face into the eyes of Lillian Walters, who was standing at the window watching them. She had been weeping.

Abruptly, Lillian Walters turned away. Standing behind her, with a face like thunder, was Thelma Braithwaite.

Thoughtfully, Mrs. Charles said good-bye to Peter and then continued on along down the drive.

As she started along the lane towards the bus stop, a woman's voice called breathlessly to her.

Mrs. Charles turned slowly and waited for Thelma Braithwaite to catch up with her.

"May I walk with you to the bus stop?" began Miss Braithwaite after a slight pause to catch her breath. "I— There's something I would like to discuss with you." She glanced at the time. "I'm afraid you've missed the four fifteen. The next bus won't be along for another half-an-hour."

"I'm not in any particular hurry," said Mrs. Charles.

"Oh," said the secretary. Then she frowned a little and added: "Good."

They had walked fifty yards or so and were almost up to the Setting Sun public house before Miss Braithwaite spoke again.

"I'm not one for pussy-footing," she said all of a rush, a flush of embarrassed colour rising on her cheeks. "I'll come straight to the point. He didn't do it: he couldn't have. We're quite frantic with worry about it. Something like this . . . well, it could ruin a person's entire life if nothing positive is done about it and it's allowed to drag on and on, which it shows every sign of doing. That's why it's so important to all of us that you—"

"Whom are you referring to, Miss Braithwaite?" the clairvoyante interrupted quietly. "To your employer or to Peter Walters?"

Thelma Braithwaite's attractive blue eyes were wide with sudden alarm. "Mr. Walters? He'd never have harmed Lorna. That was the trouble. If he'd taken a firmer stand about her right at the beginning, none of this would have happened. He was too soft: he felt sorry for her. And you can't . . . not with a girl like that, regardless of who their parents are. Give them an inch and there's no end to it! I saw the trouble coming last Christmas when she made such a pest of herself, and I warned Amery then . . . I mean Mr. Walters. I told him he was making a mistake."

"Christmas?" The clairvoyante's eyes narrowed. "Lorna Lock was here over last Christmas, too?"

"Not here at the stables, working. She had digs somewhere in Gidding, I believe: I suppose in the same lodging house that she stayed at this time. She came out here looking for Peter." A small, malicious smile flickered in the secretary's eyes. "They've got no pride, no self-respect. It's small wonder that the young men of today treat girls the way they do. And they're so persistent! She positively refused to believe us when we said that Peter wasn't here. Kept coming back and hanging around the place, making a nuisance of herself. I mean, what can one do about it?" Miss Braithwaite's eyes were wide open with indignation. "Her father's a highly-respected London physician, well-connected, plenty of money . . . One can hardly telephone the police and lodge a complaint, can one? In the end, I'm afraid that I had to be quite brutal to her—not physically, of course. Somebody had to do it . . . speak plainly to the girl about her disgraceful behaviour. Water off a duck's back, needless to say," the secretary said dourly. "She could not have cared less!"

"Peter didn't come home for Christmas?"

"No, not last year. He was very ill in hospital with glandular fever over Christmas and he went straight back to college after he was discharged."

"I see," said Mrs. Charles thoughtfully. Then, after a slight pause: "You said something a short while ago about Peter . . . that he couldn't have murdered Lorna Lock—at least, that is what I understood you to imply. Is there some special reason why he shouldn't be considered as a suspect?"

"He hurt his ankle, twisted it rather badly that morning . . . on the Saturday. He could get around, but only just. It's only been this last day or two that he's been able to move about on it properly."

"Did he have a doctor look at it?"

"No. That wasn't necessary. I bandaged it up for him. I've done a course in first aid and we get a lot of minor injuries around the stables, so I have plenty of practice with sprains and cuts and whatnot. Lorna was a strong girl . . . could work as hard as the stable-boys—and in most cases, a darn sight harder," said Miss Braithwaite dryly. "The injury that Peter had sustained to his ankle would've rendered him quite incapable of murdering her. And the way she went storming out of the house that night—"

"You were there when Mr. Walters and the girl had their disagreement?" the clairvoyante interrupted, surprised.

"I live in," the secretary explained guardedly. "Mr. and Mrs. Walters have been very kind to me since I lost my mother last year, and they both insisted that I . . . well . . ." She hesitated, then with a small frown: "You may have noticed that Mrs. Walters tends to be a rather nervy kind of person, and Mr. Walters felt that it would be good for her to have some female companionship about the place. Mrs. Walters has no interest at all in horses and racing which makes things that much more difficult for her. It's not an easy life for a woman."

Mrs. Charles reflected momentarily on the remarks that Lillian Walters had made concerning the prize-money in British horse-racing, remarks made with a fervour that one would not expect from someone as totally disinterested in the sport as Thelma Braithwaite would have her believe.

Although probably well into her forties, Thelma Braithwaite was a very attractive woman, the clairvoyante observed, one who had obviously always taken exceptionally good care of her figure and with her general appearance. The meticulously neat, fussy-looking Amery Walters would appreciate that trait in a woman, a quality which was noticeably lacking in his wife who, if one wished to be charitable, was at best rather homely.

Miss Braithwaite had gone on at some considerable length to justify her present living arrangements. When finally she paused for a breath, Mrs. Charles said:

"The argument between Mr. Walters and Lorna that night—"

"I wasn't actually in Mr. Walters' office with them," interrupted the secretary, frowning. "I was upstairs asleep in my room when Old Jack brought Lorna up to the house. The raised voices disturbed me and . . . well . . . I was startled out of a deep sleep and my first thoughts were that there was an intruder in the house and that Mr. Walters had caught the prowler red-handed. We've had a number of Saturday night burglaries—mainly, the police seem to think, because the people who commit this sort of crime quite wrongly imagine that there would be large sums of cash in the house after Mr. Walters has returned from a race meeting. Mr. Walters has never kept a lot of money about the house, so no one has ever got away with much more than a few pounds, but that hasn't deterred them one little bit: they still keep coming back on the off-chance that one night they'll get lucky."

Miss Braithwaite's eyebrows rose. "Mr. Walters has even had to buy a gun for protection. The last time that somebody broke in, Mr. Walters was dozing on his couch in the office and was taken completely by surprise . . . had to have several stitches in a deep cut on his head after the intruder had finished with him. But to get back to that Saturday night . . . Lorna. By the time I'd got my dressing gown on, it was all over. I heard the front door slam and I crossed to my window, which overlooks the side garden, and I saw her running down the drive away from the house."

"Did you go downstairs then and speak to Mr. Walters . . . ask him what the trouble was?"

"No, there was no need to: it was obvious what had happened. Lorna had been caught in one of the horse-boxes again."

"Then what happened?"

The secretary was puzzled. "I don't think I follow what you mean. . . .

"Surely an altercation of that nature must have disturbed the whole household—Mrs. Walters? Did she go downstairs to find out what all the commotion was about? If your first thoughts were that there was another intruder in the house, then surely she would've thought exactly the same thing and wouldn't have been able to turn over and go back to sleep without first having assured herself that her husband hadn't been harmed again?"

"Mrs. Walters would've drawn the same conclusion that I did . . . that it was Lorna."

"Mrs. Walters would've been able to see the girl leave, as you did?"

Miss Braithwaite frowned. "No— Her room is at the back of the house and overlooks the yard."

"*Her* room?" queried Mrs. Charles, a quizzical expression on her face.

Miss Braithwaite drew herself up a little. "Yes," she said waspishly. "*Her* room. Mrs. Walters sleeps very badly and for some time now, she's been using one of the smaller back bedrooms. Mr. Walters seldom goes to bed before two a.m. He's one of these people who require a minimum amount of sleep, and Mrs. Walter doesn't like to be disturbed when he retires for the night. Once she's awakened, she can't go back to sleep."

Mrs. Charles watched the flush of annoyed colour

rise up the secretary's neck and redden her face. Then she asked:

"Did Mrs. Walters discuss the incident with you next morning?"

"No. At least, not in any great detail. By then we had other things on our minds."

"Yes, of course," murmured Mrs. Charles. "Lorna's body had been discovered out at Beacon Point."

Miss Braithwaite started to say something, then glancing at her watch, checked herself. "I'd best be getting back," she announced abruptly. "They'll be wondering what's become of me. You shouldn't have long to wait now. . . ."

Mrs. Charles watched the secretary hurry back along the lane. And she was hurrying, Mrs. Charles mused. It was almost as if Thelma Braithwaite had allowed herself a certain amount of time with her and when that was up, like Cinderella, she had to leave or risk the consequences.

The soft purr of an engine interrupted Mrs. Charles' ruminations and she turned her head expecting that at any moment the green country bus would suddenly appear over the slight rise on the horizon.

A moment or two later, the gleaming chrome-work on a chauffeur-driven Rolls-Royce flashed brilliantly in the bright afternoon sunlight. The car was not travelling very fast and as it drew level with the woman waiting at the bus stop, the occupant of the back seat inclined his head her way and two small, very dark, deep-set eyes burned malevolently into hers. With an almost calculated arrogance, the Rolls glided on past the cricket club and the public house, then turned off the lane on to Amery Walters' drive and disappeared.

Mrs. Charles' thoughts were immediately reflected back on to the abrupt departure of Amery Walters' secretary. Thelma Braithwaite had known that her employer was about to have a visitor, had known to the precise minute when that visitor would arrive.

The clairvoyante's eyes narrowed. That urgent telephone call Amery Walters had taken a while ago . . . The late Lord Camberley's country estate would be but a short drive—no more than five or six miles, she calculated—from Amery Walters' racing stables. She had never been interested to know, nor had it ever occurred to her to wonder as to how the late life-peer's estate had been disposed of after his death; and now, she thought wryly, it was a rhetorical question. The look in the eyes of the peculiar, wizened little monkey of a man in the back seat of the Rolls-Royce was not one that she would easily forget. Rupert Roxeth had done exceedingly well for himself out of the alliance between his wife's sister and Lord Camberley: it was small wonder, mused Mrs. Charles, that Rupert Roxeth disliked her, the clairvoyante who had threatened what was probably his one and only chance of the good life.

The sun was very hot, the hedgerows hummed with the drowsy activity of the insect life they supported.

Mrs. Charles looked at the time and then shaded her eyes from the glare as she gazed along the lane. There was still no sign of a bus and she was beginning to regret not having accepted Peter Walters' offer to drive her into Gidding.

In the far off distance, walking towards her, was a man in blue denim trousers and a matching jacket. As he drew nearer, Mrs. Charles could see that he was a much younger man than she had at first thought. His fair hair, from a distance, had looked snow-white. Hanging round his neck was a pair of powerful binoculars, and he was whistling—something, Mrs. Charles reflected sadly, that one seldom heard people do these days. He sounded very happy, without a care in the world. His cheerful grin and bright 'Good afternoon' were infectious. Mrs. Charles returned his greeting with a warm smile.

The young man carried on down the lane, then suddenly he turned and retraced his steps. He was grinning as he came up to Mrs. Charles. "You wouldn't, by any chance," he said, his grin widening, "be Aunt Mary's good fairy god-mother, Mrs. Charles?"

"I don't know about the fairy god-mother part of your question, but as for the rest of it," the clairvoyante responded with a small smile, "yes, I am Edwina Charles."

The young man cocked his head to one side and eyed her quizzically. He seemed to be debating something with himself. At length, he grinned again and said, "It conjures up such romantic visions and yet . . . forgive me for saying so, but you do look more like an Edwina Charles, the archetype for what one imagines the *purr*fect English country woman to be, rather than a Madame Adele Herrmann, clairvoyante extraordinaire!"

Mrs. Charles smiled faintly. "And how would you expect Adele Herrmann to look?"

"Oh, you know," he said, flashing her a quick smile. "A bit scatty. You look far too normal and everyday to be the person that Aunt Mary and Uncle Jim enthuse about so passionately. I know," he went on in a confidential tone, narrowing his eyes, "you swallow a secret magic potion as the clock strikes twelve, and *vive la différence!*"

"You must be John," she said. "Mr. and Mrs. Sutherland's godson."

There was a violent scuffling commotion in the hedgerow directly opposite the bus stop. John turned his head towards the sound, then whistled and called:

"*Vanda, Vanda* . . . Here girl!"

A sharp yelp was followed by some more scuffling noises: then, finally, a young, part-Labrador bitch broke through the hedgerow and bounded over to them.

John made a big fuss over her. "Fool of a dog," he murmured affectionately.

The dog gazed lovingly up into his face and thumped its tail against his leg.

"Yours?" enquired Mrs. Charles, gently rubbing one of the dog's ears with her hand.

"Yes, but don't let on to Aunt Mary about it. I'll have to break the bad news to her gradually. She doesn't know it yet, but she's going to have to look after Vanda for me when I go back to college. The Walters are taking care of her for me in the meanwhile. She—Vanda—was one of a litter of four puppies that some serious-minded, highly intelligent citizen dumped on the motorway. . . ."

"You've changed your mind, then . . . about not returning to university to finish your studies?"

"Oh," he said with a fleeting smile. "They told you about that, did they?" He paused and frowned. "I never really meant it. It was something . . . well . . . I had to say it, pretend that I wasn't going back, for Peter's sake. He's going through a bad patch at the moment . . . with his father mostly. Mr. Walters only knows and understands two things, horses and horse-racing, and he won't or can't look any further than either one of them. Writing is a career for other people's sons, not his."

"He wants Peter to follow in his footsteps and become a racehorse trainer?"

John nodded. "Peter just isn't interested. He's not even all that keen on animals. He and his father have been having rows about it ever since he got home; and finally, Peter said he was throwing the lot in and going off with Roxeth—one of the owners—on an eighteen-month visit to Egypt. Roxeth is apparently going to sift the sands of the desert until he discovers the indisputable proof that the Tarot cards originated in Egypt, not Italy or in any of the other places that they are supposed to have come from. It's all Greek to me, but I understand that there are a number of schools of thought on the matter."

He paused and raised his eyebrows interrogatively, but Mrs. Charles did not comment.

"Anyway," he went on after a moment, "Roxeth—" He broke off and frowned at the clairvoyante. "You have heard of Rupert Roxeth, the so-called Tarot expert who's been helping the police with their enquiries into the Tarot murders?"

She nodded, and he then continued:

"Well, Roxeth got Peter all fired up with enthusiasm over the whole business, this controversy over the Tarot's originations, and he's now talked him into going with him out to Egypt. All expenses paid."

"Where do you fit in?"

"I don't . . . Well, I do but I don't, if you can follow my meaning," he said with a grin. "Peter is a lot like the late unlamented Lorna Lock was . . . got the same kind of temperament—the cut-off-their-nose-to-spite-their-face type. And I've found—certainly with Peter—that the quickest way to bring someone like that to their senses, is not to fight them . . . agree with them—anything they say. The more you argue with them, the more determined they become to cut off the old proboscis.

"So," he went on, sighing, "when Peter started all this nonsense about not going back to college and taking off with Roxeth instead, I simply said, 'Great: I'll come along, too. . . when do we start?' With any sort of luck, I should find that by the time the new term starts, he'll be first out of the door. No problem! Unfortunately, it's meant that I've had to carry the charade into my own life which, as you probably know, has upset my god-parents quite considerably. I did think of taking them into my confidence; but if I did do that then they wouldn't act like over-anxious parents and fret and fume, and Peter would smell a rat!"

"That's very clever of you," observed Mrs. Charles.

"Only if it works."

"You have your doubts?"

"I didn't to start with, but I have now."

"And they are?"

"In a word, Roxeth." John hesitated. Then, continuing: "Peter has changed. I can't put my finger on it, say exactly how or when the change occurred, but something's got into him. He's not himself, and I've got a horrible suspicion that he's in very real danger of letting himself be bought—literally . . . with cash! If he does what Roxeth wants—goes with him on this Egyptian sand-shifting expedition—then Roxeth will back him financially . . . help him to become a writer . . . introduce him to his influential friends."

"A tempting proposition," remarked Mrs. Charles. She studied him attentively. "Would I be right in thinking that you don't care too much for Professor Roxeth?"

He laughed. *"Professor!* What Roxeth wouldn't give to hear *you* call him that!"

"He has discussed me with you?"

"No, with Peter and Lorna. Roxeth has got, or rather *had* in Lorna's case, both of them under his spell. And do you know the impression that I got from them about Roxeth? He's frightened to death of you. You're his Achilles' heel." He fondled Vanda's ears and made loving kissing noises at her. Then he inclined his head at the racing stables. "Did you tell them that it was my Aunt Mary who wanted you to look into the Tarot murders? It's driving them out of their tiny minds not knowing. . . ."

She regarded him thoughtfully. "As you obviously know who it was, why haven't you told them?"

"And spoil the fun?" He laughed. Then, soberly: "No, that wouldn't be fair to you. They're all guilty as hell about something, and if not knowing who hired you makes someone tell the truth about that night . . . about what really happened between Lorna and Mr. Walters . . . then it's best to let things run their natural course and see what comes of it."

"Whom do you mean by 'they'?"

"All of them. Mr. and Mrs. Walters, Bossy-boots Braithwaite, Old Jack—the stable-man who caught Lorna snooping round the horse-boxes that night—and even Peter. Perhaps not so much Peter," he said after a small, reflective pause. "His edginess could be more to do with his own personal problem with his father than have anything to do with Lorna."

"Tell me about her . . . Lorna," said Mrs. Charles. "What you felt about her."

John shrugged. "I didn't like her. You couldn't like her. She was an unpleasant girl, spiteful, malicious, extremely childish . . . irritatingly so. I know she had her hang-ups—mainly over her mother . . . there was some kind of accident, I heard, which Lorna believed was her fault. But we've all got our problems," he sighed.

He paused, then frowning a little: "All the same, it was a pretty unpleasant way for anyone to go. And when I found her . . . you know, realised that it was Lorna and not just some strange woman floating there in the water, I felt really sorry—guilty. We all did . . . all the lads. We didn't realise then that she'd been murdered. We naturally thought that her mind had finally flipped and that she'd walked deliberately into the sea and put an end to it all. As we rode out that morning, Peter told me about the argument that she'd had with his father the previous night, and that Mr. Walters had told her to get out and not to come back. To me—to all of us, in fact—that just seemed like the final straw. Murder never entered our heads. And yet," he said reflectively, "in retrospect, it's surprising that it didn't: I mean, all of us knowing so well what she used to be like with everyone. She never knew how far to go and when to stop. Someone like her . . . well, one day they're bound to play out their line too far."

"When she left Mr. Walters' house that night, how would she have got back to her digs . . . assuming, of course, that that was her intention?"

John thought for a moment. "By the bus, I suppose."

"Wouldn't it have been too late for that?"

He hesitated. "I'm not sure. I think I remember someone once saying that the last bus leaves shortly before midnight. I don't know if that means from here, this stop, or from Hetley Vale. It was the bus from Hetley Vale, the one you're waiting for, that she sometimes used to catch back to her digs in Gidding. If the bus leaves from Hetley Vale just before midnight, then according to what Peter told me, Lorna would've been in plenty of time to have caught it. I've never done the journey by bus myself, but it must take it at least half-an-hour if not longer to get from Hetley Vale to Mr. Walters' stables."

"The argument between Mr. Walters and Lorna, I understand, took place somewhere around midnight. . . ."

"So I believe. Peter told me that he was on his way to relieve Old Jack, who was on guard duty up to twelve, when Old Jack caught Lorna snooping about the place and made her go along with him to see Mr. Walters."

"What do you think Lorna was doing near the horse-boxes at that hour of night?"

"I don't know for sure, but I'd be willing to risk a guess. She'd got wind of something unpleasant and she wanted to see for herself if it was true."

"She was concerned that one of Professor Roxeth's horses might have been ill-treated?"

He gave the clairvoyante a quick, penetrating look. "You haven't wasted any time, I see." His expression soured. "Despicable little toad!" he muttered through clenched teeth.

"Rupert Roxeth?"

He shrugged irritably. "How I'd like to give him a taste of his own medicine."

"Is it at all likely that Lorna, after her illicit visit to the horse-boxes that night and her consequent quarrel with Mr. Walters, might've felt that way, too?"

He frowned. "You mean that after she left Mr. Walters, she went out to Roxeth's place?" He looked doubtful. "It's the sort of thing that Lorna would do if she were mad enough, but somehow I don't think she would've been . . . angry enough with Roxeth, I mean. Mr. Walters wouldn't come at what Roxeth wanted him to do with the horse."

"Didn't that then mean that Professor Roxeth would take the horse away from the stables and have it slaughtered?"

"That was his threat, but I doubt that he's *that* stupid. The horse is too good and Roxeth knows it."

"Do you know what Mr. Walters and Lorna said to one another that night?"

He shook his head. "Mr. Walters is supposed to have booted her out . . . you know, for defying him and going near the horses, but I don't know—" He paused and gazed thoughtfully at the Labrador which was foraging busily in the long dry grass growing on the verge of the lane. "Things were never that simple with Lorna. An argument could start on one thing and end up on something totally different. She had a knack of dragging everything up and of somehow making it relevant to whatever the current squabble was about. She was a very strange girl," he said abstractedly. "Had absolutely no sense of right or wrong . . . of what was fair play and what was hitting way below the belt. If she had a point to get across, she'd use any means whatever to ensure that it got home. You had to be very careful around her, watch what you said and how you behaved. She was pretty astute and that made her dangerous, *very* dangerous."

"In other words, Lorna had discovered, or guessed, that there is a somewhat more intimate relationship between Mr. Walters and his secretary than that of employer and employee."

He cocked an eyebrow at her. "You're another one who is pretty astute and therefore probably very dangerous. No wonder they're quaking at the knees ... Although it's fairly obvious what's going on—Mrs. Walters in tears most of the time and Miss Braithwaite needling Mr. Walters to do something positive about the situation ... like hand Mrs. Walters her hat and coat and show her to the front door. Which he can't do. It's her front door. Peter told me that his father put everything in his mother's name ... years ago, when Mr. Walters first started training racehorses. Peter didn't say why, but I presume it was a safeguard in case things didn't pan out the way Mr. Walters hoped and he was threatened with bankruptcy and in danger of losing the house and the stables."

"A most unpleasant situation," murmured Mrs. Charles.

"Particularly for Mrs. Walters." He paused, frowning. "She doesn't deserve it, to be treated the way Mr. Walters is treating her. And that's the sort of thing I meant about Lorna. Something like that—Mr. Walters' affair with his secretary ... Lorna would take it and use it against them without a second thought about what she was doing to Mrs. Walters, the innocent party. And even if she did realise that she was hurting her as well, she wouldn't care. Lorna just didn't give a damn. You got in her way at your own peril." His eyes widened expressively. "She gave me a few scares, and I don't mind admitting it."

"Ah yes," said the clairvoyante pensively. "The pitchfork."

"Vanda! Vanda!" he called out abruptly. "Not where the horses have been . . . there's a good girl."

With a quick, apologetic smile at Mrs. Charles, he then said, "I'm sorry: you were saying? Oh yes, the pitchfork. My own fault. I should've known better, but it was just one of those unguarded moments. She walked into the shed where I was working—looking as if she'd just gone fifteen rounds with Muhammad Ali . . . all black round the eyes from lack of sleep, her face dirty, hair standing on end, her clothes filthy and torn—and I simply said what I was thinking, spoke my thoughts out loud. I honestly think she would've stuck the pitchfork right through me if it hadn't been for Peter and the others. Luckily, Peter was on his way out to talk to me about something and was only a few yards away when she went for me."

"Was she fond of him?"

"Of Peter?" The question took him by surprise: the thought had obviously never occurred to him. He was quiet for a few moments, considering the possibility. Then he said, "Well, all I can say is that if she did fancy him, then she had a very peculiar way of showing it."

"There's not even the slightest possibility that she might've been secretly in love with him?"

He shook his head slowly. "No way—"

"I see," said Mrs. Charles, nodding her head thoughtfully. "You spoke a moment ago of Peter and

Lorna being under Professor Roxeth's spell. What did you mean?"

"Exactly that— He hypnotised the two of them. I could never understand it myself—see what they saw in him." He widened his eyes and raised his shoulders in a gesture of complete bewilderment. "They hung on to every word he said, and yet as far as I'm concerned, I've never heard such puerile twaddle from one so allegedly highly educated."

"Lorna and Peter spent a lot of time in his company?"

"Roxeth likes having young people round him," he said dryly. "It's all part of the illusion he has about himself. Next to being afraid of you, he's terrified of growing old, and by having young people about him all the time, he sees himself as he sees them. I'd feel sorry for him if only he weren't so obnoxious. Unfortunately," he went on with a crooked smile, "like Lorna, Roxeth is so unpleasant that it's impossible to be big about him and feel any real pity for him."

"You speak of him as though you too spend a good deal of time in his company."

His very fair eyebrows came close together in an intense frown. "Peter is a very good writer . . . got loads of natural talent. He doesn't need Roxeth. He'll make it without having to compromise himself to anyone. If Roxeth were any other kind of man, I mightn't feel so strongly about Peter throwing up his chance of graduating with an arts degree: but in the circumstances, Roxeth being what he is, I'd be no sort of friend at all if I didn't make some attempt to prevent Peter from making the kind of mistake which I think he'll finish up regretting for the rest of his life. So where Peter goes, I go . . . that's if Roxeth is going to be anywhere about the place."

"He's there now, at the stables," said Mrs. Charles.

The fair eyebrows shot up. "Roxeth? Good lord . . . that was quick! How did they send out the distress call? Tom-tom? Or did they use smoke signals?" He chuckled. "There must be a right old flap going on back there. Roxeth is like an excitable monkey when he gets worked up about something. Dances about screeching and tearing out his hair. I honestly think he's mad, you know . . . right round the jolly old twist!" He inclined his head to one side and regarded her curiously. "I don't suppose there's any chance that you will get the better of him?"

"In what way?"

"Over the Tarot . . . his interpretation of the cards —you know, all that pretentious mumbo-jumbo he's told the police about the meanings of the cards the Tarot murderer left with Lorna and that other girl."

"Professor Roxeth is a recognised expert on the Tarot. I would be the last person to quarrel with his findings."

His eyes slowly widened. "Does that mean you agree with what Mr. Sayer has told Aunt Mary and Uncle Jim about Roxeth's belief that the two cards point to the identity of the Tarot murderer?"

"The cards have many different meanings. One person may interpret a card one way, and another may see its meaning as something entirely different, yet both may be correct."

He studied her for a moment, then made a small face. "Looks like I might've owed Roxeth an apology. That would be if," he added, grinning, "I'd ever told him what I thought of him and all the boring nonsense that he used to talk to Lorna and Peter about the Tarot."

"Would you say that Peter has become deeply interested in the Tarot?"

He gave her a startled look. "I hope not! Lord knows where it will end if he starts taking Roxeth too seriously."

"What about Lorna?"

He shrugged carelessly. "Lorna was a listener . . . that is, for the most part. She never let on what she was thinking or how she felt about something until she was ready to let fly; and then she'd really give it to you, let you have it with everything she'd got . . . all the little bits of information that she'd stored up, any observations she'd made, would suddenly pour forth from her like a torrential cloudburst and you'd be left battered and bruised and wondering what on earth had hit you."

"You can't remember her ever discussing the Tarot?"

"Not in my presence."

"Do you know if she owned a pack of Tarot cards?"

He shook his head. "Why do you ask?"

"I'm merely curious to know how interested she was in the Tarot."

"That would be anyone's guess," he said. "You never knew for sure just why she'd be interested in anything. She was a great one for ulterior motives was our Lorna."

He shaded his eyes with both hands and gazed along the lane. "Here comes your bus now," he observed. He whistled to the dog and called, "Here girl."

Vanda raised her head and stared thoughtfully at

the two human beings, then wandered leisurely up to John who took her securely by the collar and drew her with him well over on to the verge clear of the roadway. As Mrs. Charles stepped aboard the bus, he grinned up at her and said: "Good-bye and good luck!"

Mrs. Charles moved unsteadily to the rear of the lurching conveyance and took up a seat where she could watch John until he was lost to her in the distance. He was standing in the middle of the lane with the binoculars to his eyes watching a sparrow-hawk.

The narrow white card beneath the bellpush confirmed that this, the garden-flat, No. 12 Roedene Close, was indeed occupied by Miss Karen Wheeler.

Mrs. Charles depressed the bellpush and after a very long wait, the door was finally opened by a young, flaxen-haired girl in a flower-patterned bikini. A striped bath towel was slung carelessly over one shoulder and in her right hand was a romantic paperback novel and a bottle of suntan lotion.

"Miss Wheeler?" enquired Mrs. Charles.

"Karen's not in at the moment," the girl replied in a soft Irish brogue.

"Oh," said Mrs. Charles. "Never mind. I happened to be in Gidding this afternoon and I just called round on the off-chance that I would find her in. Mrs. Noad gave me her address."

"Miriam's mum?" the girl asked, surprised.

"Yes." Mrs. Charles' eyebrows rose interrogatively. "You knew Miriam?"

The girl nodded. "We were doing our training together . . . at the hospital round the corner—Gidding General." She looked at her watch. "Karen finishes at five thirty and it's just that now. She'll be in at any moment if you'd like to come in and wait. I was just going to put the kettle on for a cup of tea and you look as if you could use one."

"Yes," agreed Mrs. Charles. "I have had a busy day."

The girl led the way into a room so overcrowded

with odd pieces of furniture and the knick-knackery of the young that one automatically paused on passing through the doorway to speculate on where best to seat oneself.

"Sorry I kept you waiting at the door," she apologised brightly, "but I was right down at the bottom of the garden getting some sun." She gathered up an armful of unironed underwear from the settee and deposited it on another pile of freshly-laundered clothing on an ironing-board. "Make yourself comfortable," she invited. "I won't be a jiff." She disappeared momentarily, then suddenly her head shot round the door and she said, "By the way, my name is Rosemary (Rosie to my friends) McAfee *hyphen* Smith. It's a scream, isn't it . . . the hyphen?" she added with a pert grin. And off she went back to the kitchen, the hall echoing with her mirth.

Five minutes later, she returned with a tray of tea and sweet biscuits. She had slipped on a pair of patched, faded blue jeans, the legs of which had been roughly hacked off an inch or two above the knee where they were badly frayed. The white blouse she was now wearing was knotted at the front revealing a bare, suntanned midriff.

"How is Mrs. Noad?" she enquired.

"Still very distressed."

"Ah, the poor woman," murmured Rosie sympathetically. She poured a cup of tea and passed it to Mrs. Charles. "Are you a friend of the family?"

"No." Mrs. Charles leaned back against the settee and studied the young Irish girl meditatively. "I am what might be called an interested observer."

"*Uh huh!*" said Rosie with feeling. "I might've guessed that it would be one or the other—a snoop or a crackpot!" She eyed Mrs. Charles curiously. "You don't *look* like a crackpot—not that it's that easy to tell, mind . . . the nuttiest of nutters are often the sanest of people to look at. But then again, neither can you be a snoop because Mrs. Noad wouldn't have given you this address."

Rosie bit thoughtfully into a biscuit and munched it slowly. She went on: "My stars for today said that I was going tto meet someone very interesting . . . someone who was going to leave an indelible impression on me. I must confess that I was hoping for a fellah, but not to worry. Carry on . . . make your indelible impression."

"You are interested in such things—fortune-telling?"

"Isn't everyone?"

"Was Miriam?"

Rosie shrugged. "Not especially. Why do you ask?"

"As a clairvoyante, I am naturally interested to know these things."

"Oh," groaned Rosie. "Bingo!" She shook her head sadly. "And me letting you in."

"You have been unduly pestered by such people?" enquired Mrs. Charles imperturbably.

"Oh, I wouldn't be saying that now," the girl said dryly. "It's had its lighter moments. Like the weirdo who turned up with a forked stick—something like a water divining-rod—and wanted to go all over the flat with it, using it like a vacuum cleaner, to pick up Miriam's astral vibrations which he claimed would then lead him straight to her killer."

"My interest is principally in the Tarot."

The girl hesitated, only very briefly, but the slowness to respond did not pass unnoticed. "Well, that's something," she sighed. "The first we've had of that lot!"

She regarded Mrs. Charles quizzically. "You're quite sure that it was Mrs. Noad who gave you this address?"

"Quite sure. I visited her at her home in Hetley Vale yesterday afternoon."

There was an odd look on Rosie's face. "Mrs. Noad talked to *you* . . . about *Miriam*?"

"When she realised who I was, yes."

The girl widened her eyes at the clairvoyante. "Well, don't keep me in suspense. Who are you?"

"I am known as Edwina Charles, but my real name is Adele Herrmann."

The girl's eyes lingered momentarily on the clairvoyante's beringed fingers. "Oh," she responded. "I've never heard of either one of you."

"No," said the other woman. "I daresay you haven't. It was a little while ago now, but I was once involved in a murder investigation in which the Tarot played a small part."

"How do you mean '*involved*'?"

"In every sense of the word. I was both accused and accuser."

"You mean that everyone thought you did it, but you didn't and found out who did?"

"Something like that."

"And Mrs. Noad knew all about it?"

"The matter was reported very fully at the time in most of the local newspapers."

The girl considered Mrs. Charles very thoughtfully. Then, after a moment or two, she said, "Okay. If Mrs. Noad trusts you, that's good enough for me. Have another cup of tea, Mrs. Herrmann."

"*Madame* Herrmann," the clairvoyante corrected her with a grave smile.

"Oops," said the girl with a giggle. "My mistake. Sorry."

She refilled Mrs. Charles' cup. Then, suddenly very serious, she said, "Could the cards tell you who murdered Miriam and that other girl?"

"It is not impossible. However, that is not my expectation. The Tarot murderer will tell me who he—or she—is."

Rosie was pouring herself another cup of tea which she slopped badly in the saucer. She frowned at Mrs. Charles.

"He—or she—won't be able to help himself," the clairvoyante went on unconcernedly, aware of the impact that she was having on the girl but not looking directly at her. "The Tarot murderer thinks himself very clever, too clever to be caught and that, ultimately, will be his—or her—downfall."

"You keep saying 'he or she'," observed Rosie nervously. "The Tarot murderer could be a woman?"

"I see no reason why not. I would say that it's about fifty-fifty, wouldn't you . . . the ratio of murders committed by one sex as compared with the other?"

Rosie stirred her tea, a thoughtful expression on her face.

"I hadn't thought of it like that," she said slowly. "You know, that it could be a woman. And yet . . . Well, in one way it makes sense—that the Tarot murderer is a woman. I never could understand why Miriam got into a car with a strange man. She didn't do silly things like that. But a strange woman . . . who'd think twice? We're all conditioned from the time we're quite small children to think that it's the men who are the villains, but an evil woman can be just as bad. Sometimes a sight worse." She was quiet for a moment, thinking. Then she frowned and said, "I know it's none of my business—and you can tell me so if you want to . . . I won't mind," she assured Mrs. Charles earnestly. "But what do you want to see Karen about?"

Mrs. Charles considered the question for a very long time before responding to it.

"There is some reason for your question? There was, perhaps, some animosity between Miriam and Karen?"

Rosie sighed and flopped back in her chair, arms and legs askew. She remained in that position for several moments, then she sighed again and straightened up a little.

"The police asked me—all of Miriam's friends—the same thing . . . not specifically about Karen, of course —and we all more or less gave the same answer. None of us could think of anything . . . you know, any unpleasantness. Shock, I suppose. I know my mind went completely blank. For days afterwards, all I could think was, *Miriam's dead . . . murdered!* But, well, now that you mention it . . . Karen and Miriam." She clasped her hands in front of her and gazed at them intently. "It's hard now to say why, how or even when it started—"

"Somewhere around last Christmas?" suggested Mrs. Charles.

Rosie looked up at her in surprise. "Yes . . . It would've been somewhere around then." She paused reflectively. Then, continuing:

"We—some of the nursing staff—had a bit of a 'do' at the Crown. Karen was invited . . . she's not on the nursing staff, but she's pretty friendly with most of the girls in our little clique and she's usually included in everything that we do together. Anyway, sometime during the evening, I went out to the 'Ladies' and walked in on the two of them having a blazing row. They hushed up when they saw me come in, but you could tell what had been going on. You could've cut the air with a knife! I said something to them—what I can't remember—and then went into the loo. When I came out, they'd gone back to our table and were carrying on as if nothing had happened."

"You didn't hear any of their quarrel?"

"No. It was just obvious that they'd been at one another's throats. I'd always been fairly friendly with the two of them, but not that friendly that I could . . . well, you know, ask what the hell was going on!"

"Neither one of them ever referred to the incident?"

"No. But . . ." Rosie hesitated, a distant look in her eye. Then she went on: "Sometimes I wonder if it wasn't all in my imagination, but I never felt that after that night things were ever quite the same between them."

"Do you have any idea at all what they might've been quarrelling about?"

"Yeah, sure . . . A fellah, of course. Had to be, didn't it? What else do young, healthy, competitive females have to fight about?"

"There were young men with you that evening?"

"No. It was a hens' party. All cackle and scratch-scratch," said the girl with a grin.

"You don't know who the young man might've been?"

"*If* there ever was one," said Rosie. "No."

"You've since changed your mind about the cause of Miriam and Karen's quarrel?"

"Yes and no. My natural female instinct tells me

that there was a fellah involved, but then," said Rosie, widening her eyes at Mrs. Charles, "Miriam wasn't *that* interested. She liked fellahs . . . always had a good time, but she had other higher priorities and getting serious about one fellah and married and tied down to a house and kids wasn't one of them. She wanted very badly to be a theatre sister, and I think that when she'd done that, achieved her ambition, then that was when she'd have started thinking about getting serious about a fellah. But it would've had to be someone in the medical profession—a doctor . . . someone who'd understand how important her nursing career was to her. Miriam could be very . . ." Rosie searched for the right word. "*Calculating!* Yes, that's how she was. There was a time and a place for everything and everything in its time and place. Very nice, too—if you can arrange it, your life, like that."

"Which she didn't," observed Mrs. Charles.

"No," agreed Rosie. "Something went very badly wrong somewhere along the line. And yet . . ." She made a small face and shrugged. "Things just didn't go wrong for Miriam. She was too much of a strategist. That makes her sound tough and hard-boiled, but she wasn't. I think that what it was with Miriam was that whereas it takes some people years—a lifetime sometimes—to know what they want and what their limitations are, Miriam always knew exactly what she wanted from life and how far she could stretch herself. She never over-reached herself and consequently, anything and everything she took on—like Miss Gidding General—she won hands down."

Mrs. Charles' eyebrows rose. "Miriam won the Miss Gidding General competition?"

Rosie nodded. "The summer fete next Saturday—

that was when Miriam was to have been crowned. The 'do' we had—the one I was talking about a few moments ago . . . it was a sort of discussion—committee meeting, if you like—about it. We decided that this year the entrants in the contest would raise funds for a mobile kidney dialysis machine."

"Miriam and Karen were both on this fund raising committee?"

"Initially, yes. Then they decided to become competitors and they both pulled out of the organising side of it."

"And Miriam won," said the clairvoyante musingly.

"Naturally." The girl grinned good-naturedly. "Karen raised the next highest amount of money, so she gets to wear the sash and crown on Saturday. We had a meeting about it after Miriam was murdered . . . you know, to decide whether or not to drop the Miss Gidding General presentation from the fete this year in view of what had happened to Miriam, but we— the Miss Gidding General committee and Lady Felton, the fete organiser—finally decided that it wouldn't be fair to the others, the runners-up. It seemed a shame to shelve it after they'd all worked so hard. . . ."

"Quite," said Mrs. Charles. "A fund raising competition of this kind must have placed a very heavy burden on Miriam . . . what with her studies and her other commitments."

"Miriam took everything in her stride, especially hard work. She thrived on it. And she'd never have taken on the Miss Gidding General contest if she'd thought she couldn't cope and that it would interfere with her training."

"Her mother, when I spoke to her yesterday, expressed the opinion that she felt that Miriam's studies were proving to be too much for her, that she was having a bit of a struggle to keep up."

Rosie seemed surprised. "Did she?"

"You would disagree with her?"

The girl shrugged. "Miriam's mum should know . . . but, well, that's the first I've heard of it."

"Wasn't Miriam sent home by the hospital authorities for a rest?"

"Yes, but that was because she'd been ill. There was a very nasty upper respiratory infection going round the nursing staff and she went down with it and it flattened her . . . hit her harder than the rest of us, and she didn't seem to pick up after it—lost weight, didn't want to eat . . . the usual post 'flu depression: so she was packed off home for a good rest. But that was all there was to it . . .That is, as far as I know," Rosie admitted.

"Her work was affected?"

"She was badly run-down, tired, very nervy—which wasn't at all like Miriam. No one can do their job properly in that condition."

"No," agreed Mrs. Charles. She paused. Then, narrowing her eyes: "Miriam's mother also seemed concerned about the effect that Miriam's social work was having on her. Mrs. Noad felt that it was too depressing for Miriam and that it was getting her down."

"The Good Samaritan?"

As she considered the possibility, Rosie's pale blue eyes grew slowly wider and rounder. "I never noticed it. There's plenty there to get depressed about, mind you. If that's your nature."

"You help out there, too?"

"Yes. They roped me in."

"They?"

"Miriam and Karen."

"Miriam never expressed any feeling of despair over the problems suffered by the people who go to The Good Samaritan for help?"

"Despair never helped anyone to get well and Miriam knew that better than most. She felt for people and she cared about others—anyone less fortunate than herself . . . that was why she was a nurse and it was also what took her to The Good Samaritan in the first place. But she never wasted any of her time and energy on useless emotion. She was too much of a professional to make that mistake."

Mrs. Charles studied Rosie contemplatively. "I am puzzled," the clairvoyante confessed at length, "about Mrs. Noad's conviction that when she visited Miriam over Christmas, there was something on Miriam's mind, something depressing her, and that her nursing training and the social work she did for The Good Samaritan were behind it. Can you think of anything, any incident—no matter how small—which occurred at either the hospital or The Good Samaritan over Christmas which might've upset Miriam in some way?"

Rosie shook her head. "I'm sorry . . . can't help you there, I'm afraid. I didn't get roped in until March. I've only been helping out at The Good Samaritan for a few months. Karen would know, though—Ask her."

"Yes," said Mrs. Charles. "I shall . . . But what about the hospital? Did anything untoward take place there over the Christmas period? Was there some dissension, perhaps, amongst the nursing staff?"

Rosie was shaking her head very slowly. "No, nothing that I can think of." She hesitated, thought for a moment, then gave a quick shake of her head and said, "No, that wouldn't have upset her: Miriam didn't give a damn for possessions, or 'inanimates', as she called them. And she herself said it was only worth a few pounds."

"She lost something?"

Rosie pulled a wry face. "Quite a few of us did . . . the nursing staff and some of the patients. Only we didn't exactly *lose* our things, if you know what I mean."

"They were pilfered?"

The girl nodded.

"What was stolen from Miriam?"

"The same sort of thing . . . jewellery. An initial necklet, I think Karen said. I never actually discussed it with Miriam: I heard about it through Karen, and as far as I know, Miriam never even reported the loss officially. The necklet wasn't an expensive one, so she apparently felt that it wasn't worth all the fuss and bother of reporting its loss."

"Was it recovered?"

"No. None of us ever got anything back. They never found the thief, either. The hospital authorities brought in a security adviser and that was the end of the pilfering: the thief obviously got to hear of it and was scared off."

Rosie paused, then went on musingly: "About The Good Samaritan . . . I think you're barking up the wrong tree there. Miriam never got that emotionally involved . . . with people, I mean."

"There was no one in whom she took a particular interest?"

"Not to my knowledge. Only Scottie. But then," said Rosie with a small shrug, "we all cared about old Scottie."

"*Old* Scottie? I thought The Good Samaritan was concerned with young people."

"Yes, and so it is: but we get our share of the others, people like Scottie . . . ladies and gentlemen of the road."

"Drifters?"

Rosie nodded. "Scottie has a bit of a drink problem as well. A real character, though. He hasn't been around for a while. Reverend Povey—he runs The Good Samaritan—was going to have a word to the police about him . . . y'know, in case something has happened to him and he's lying hurt somewhere. We thought he'd drifted off up North, back home to Scotland, but nobody we've asked about him has seen him on any of the roads. But he'll turn up. They usually do . . . when you least expect it."

"Was there any special way in which Miriam expressed her interest in this man? Did she do more for him than she did for anyone else?"

"Oh no," said Rosie quickly. "Miriam never had favourites, not in that way. She treated everyone the same. Scottie, like I've said—was a bit of a character . . . interesting to talk to—when he wasn't in his cups. He'd obviously had a better than average education. He could talk on any subject you cared to mention, quite authoritively, too, though never at any great length." She made a small face. "The demon drink, I'm afraid . . . damaged his brain. He'd talk for a while, lucidly and quite intelligently, and then his mind would suddenly slip away and he'd just sit there, staring at nothing, in a little befuddled world of his own. He was very clever with his hands: he used to do these wood carvings . . . bring them along to The Good Samaritan to show us. I think that's how he got the money for the drink: he'd sell them on the road. Did a very nice one for Miriam . . . as a present. For a surprise. She was really choked about it."

"What do you mean by 'choked'?"

"You know . . . all emotional, in tears. It wasn't like her to display that kind of emotion," said the girl reflectively, "but then that was when she wasn't feeling her best after the chest infection."

"This happened somewhere around the time that she was sent home by the hospital for a rest?"

"Yes. That week. Scottie came in with the picture on the Wednesday and she was packed off home on the Friday."

"Where is the picture now . . . with her mother?"

"No, it's hanging on the bedroom wall. Mrs. Noad said that Karen could have it. I'll show it to you."

Rosie disappeared. She obviously had some difficulty dislodging the picture from the wall for there was a scraping noise and a loud bump as if something had fallen on to the floor followed by some mild cursing. Eventually she returned.

The wood carving, which was beautifully framed, was smaller than Mrs. Charles had imagined it would be—roughly five inches long by three, she guessed.

"Nice, isn't it?" said Rosie.

"Have you any idea what it's meant to depict?" enquired Mrs. Charles.

"Oh yes, sure I do. Karen told me. It's *The Tower of Destruction,* isn't it? From the Tarot."

XII   THE HANGED MAN
A Life in Suspension

The front door opened and closed. "That'll be Karen now," said Rosie quickly, taking the picture from Mrs. Charles. "Just excuse me for a moment. I won't be long."

A few minutes later, Karen Wheeler entered the room alone. Her flat-mate had obviously satisfied her as to their visitor's bona fides for she said, simply, "Good evening. My friend said you wanted to speak to me about Miriam."

Karen was, thought Mrs. Charles, an extremely pretty girl. Chestnut-haired, twenty-one or there-abouts, had good taste in clothes—nothing about her, the smart well-cut suit, the pure silk blouse, her soft feminine hair-style, had that thrown-together-at-the-moment look which young people nowadays strove to achieve and seemed to consider the height of fashion.

She sat down in a chair opposite Mrs. Charles and crossed her slim legs. Her hands were folded neatly in her lap in an attitude which the longer Mrs. Charles studied her, became all the more offensively patron-ising. The girl's clear green eyes, though, told a very different story. They were watchful, calculating. She was the kind of person who would say one thing and invariably mean something else again. A girl, Mrs. Charles decided, whom she would not care to trust.

"What was it you wished to know?" Karen enquired without interest.

Quite suddenly, all the questions which Mrs. Charles had intended to ask Karen, became irrelevant. The impression which she had formed of the girl became stronger. She was wasting her time. Karen Wheeler would not tell her what she wanted to know.

"You look tired, my dear," said the clairvoyante quietly. "I won't trouble you now. It was nothing important." She rose from the settee. "Please thank your friend for the tea for me."

With almost bored disinterest, Karen watched the clairvoyante leave. Reaching the door, Mrs. Charles paused and looked back across the disordered room. The complete lie, she thought. That neat, coolly efficient girl in all that dreadful muddle. . . .

"I believe congratulations are in order for Saturday," she said. "I wish you a very happy day."

Rosie's head popped round the door. "What happened? Did you throw her out?" she asked wide-eyed.

Karen shrugged her shoulders. "A bit of a case, like you said. She simply congratulated me about Saturday and walked out."

The other girl came right into the room. "That's funny." She gazed at Karen, a thoughtful expression on her face. "I wonder . . . Do you ever get the feeling that you've opened your mouth and put your foot in it?"

"What do you mean?"

"I'm not sure, but I've got a feeling that I've gone and done it again."

"Done what?" asked Karen, sighing impatiently.

"Talked too much." Rosie hesitated. Then she shuddered and wrapped her arms tightly about herself. "I feel like . . . you know, as if somebody just walked over my grave. You don't suppose she could do it, do you? Find out who the Tarot murderer is?"

"Of course not. Don't be silly."

"She's no fool, Karen."

"That's not what you told me out in the kitchen."
Karen's mouth twisted into an ugly shape and the
green eyes glittered vindictively. "'*A right case*'," she
mimicked the other girl. "Wasn't that what you said?"

"It's just that . . . well, she's got the knack of getting you going. You don't realise it at the time . . ."
Rosie bit her bottom lip and gave Karen an anxious
look. "It's as well you got home when you did. Lord
knows what I would've told her if I had been left
alone with her much longer."

Karen stared intently into the other girl's eyes,
then her gaze lowered to the object in her right hand.

"What are you doing with that?" she asked sharply.

"I'm just going to put it back on the bedroom
wall."

"What is it doing out here?"

"I showed it to her, didn't I?"

"You did *what*?"

"We were talking about Scottie and I . . . well . . .
I showed it to her," said Rosie defensively. "She was
interested . . ."

"*Interested!*" Karen snapped at her irritably. "You
little fool! You know what that carving was taken
from."

"Yes . . . the Tarot. You told me."

"So what if she goes to the police and tells them
about it . . . after we told them that Miriam knew
nothing about the Tarot?"

"But that was true. Miriam didn't know anything
about fortune-telling."

"Where do you think Scottie got the idea in the
first place for making a carving of *The Tower of*

Destruction? From the same bolt of lightning that strikes the tower?" asked Karen sarcastically.

Rosie's eyes were enormous in her face which had paled beneath its tan. "I didn't give it any thought—"

"Well, I suggest you do. Right now!"

"You don't have to bite my head off! I didn't mean any harm." Abashed, Rosie turned to leave. Then, suddenly angry with the other girl, she swung round at her and said, "You know you're getting to be as irritable and nervy as Miriam was!" she flounced over to the door. "And as big a pain in the neck!"

Mrs. Charles had hesitated for quite some considerable time before telephoning David Sayer. She had felt that it was too soon . . . She had really very little for him and was not yet ready to commit herself to the reading of the cards involved in the two Tarot murders which James and Mary Sutherland had requested of her. Not because she was unsure of herself. She knew now exactly what *The Star* and *The Moon* meant, their full significance, and yet she felt strangely dissatisfied with her findings, as if this knowledge were not enough and she should be patient, hold on to what she knew for just a short while longer. In expectation of what, she was not sure. And now there was no time for speculation. Not if she were to prevent the Tarot murderer from striking again.

She apologized to David for having asked him to drive over to the village from Gidding so late at night. "But I felt," she then went on to explain as they crossed the hall to the sitting-room and sat down, "that what I wished to discuss with you would be better said to you in person. One gets so many crossed lines these days," she sighed, "and I wouldn't want to alarm anyone."

"That all sounds rather ominous," he observed, eyeing her curiously. Mrs. Charles wasn't what he termed 'a panic merchant'. If she were worried about something, worried enough to drag him from his home at this late hour of night, then it was with good reason.

"I have been sitting here for an hour or more, trying to make up my mind," she confessed absently. "I know what is going to happen and yet I suspect, *strongly* suspect that I am powerless, that there is nothing that I can do about it. Death is an inevitability which faces each and every one of us: an untimely death is an altogether different matter. It can be avoided, Superintendent," she said with an earnest frown. *"But only if one has co-operation . . ."*

Abruptly, she got to her feet and went over to the writing bureau in a far corner of the room, removed something from it, then returned to the sofa and sat down again. In her right hand was a pack of Tarot cards.

"Let me show you something, Superintendent," she said quietly.

She spent a minute or two sorting through the cards: then, finally, she laid a card on the round occasional table which separated them and looked up at him.

"There," she said, "we have Miriam Noad. Tarot victim No. 1. *The Star.*"

David went to get up to come round to her side of the table, but she stopped him.

"No, please stay where you are, Superintendent. I am laying out the cards as they would be placed were you the seeker. In other words, to read them, I (the clairvoyante) would be the one to move. You'll notice," she went on, "that at the moment, the card is the correct way up—you can see exactly what card it is . . . that it is card number seventeen, a symbolic picture card from the Major Arcana of the Tarot, *The Star.* Now watch . . ."

Mrs. Charles leaned forward and twisted the card round. *"The Star* is now what is known as *inverted—*

I (the clairvoyante) can read it, see clearly which card it is, but you (the seeker) cannot . . . not without craning your neck. That, Superintendent, is the way *The Star* was left by the Tarot murderer on Miriam Noad's body. *Inverted.*"

"Yes," he said, nodding his head slowly. "I talked to a friend of mine down at police headquarters early this morning, like you suggested, and he said that *The Star* was definitely upside down—or 'inverted', as you say—on Miriam Noad's body when she was found . . . upside-down to her, that is. There's some doubt about the card with Lorna Lock's body . . . which way round it was. John Carrington-Jones couldn't remember. But one of the lads who rode out with him that morning said he watched John unzip Lorna's wind-cheater and then toss the card aside as he got down to the business of trying to resuscitate her, and this young lad seems to think that it was the right way up . . . If Lorna had been alive and able to raise her head to look at it, she would've seen instantaneously which card it was. I phoned you this afternoon to tell you what I'd learned and tried again—"

He pulled himself up short. "How did you find out about the card with Miriam Noad's body?"

Concealing her amusement at the expression on his face, one that she had come to know so well, the clairvoyante said, "By reading the card which preceded it."

He stared at her blankly. "I don't follow you . . ."

She leaned forward again and placed another symbolic picture card from the Major Arcana, *The Tower of Destruction,* immediately to the left of *The Star.*

"*The Tower of Destruction,* upright," she murmured, "followed by *The Star,* inverted. A combination of cards, Superintendent, which has a special significance and tells me quite a lot about the Tarot murderer."

He started to say something, but she held up a hand and said, "Bear with me for a few moments longer, Superintendent. Then I will answer all your questions."

"Now," she went on, "we come to Tarot victim No. 2. Lorna Lock." She laid another card on the table to the right of the other two. "*The Moon,* upright," she said. "Mr. Walters' stable-boy was quite correct—"

David interrupted. "John told Mary—Mary Sutherland—that you'd been out to Walters' place today and that you'd spoken to him. You managed to jog John's memory?"

"No. We didn't discuss the card at all. There was no need to . . . I have always been confident about which way round that card was because of this card, Superintendent, *Justice,* which preceded it." She laid that card, *Justice,* on the table to the left of *The Moon* and then looked up at him expectantly.

He ran his eye over these two cards, then frowned at her. "This is another special combination?"

"Some consider it so."

"You don't?"

She smiled a little. "Let me give you a very brief history of the Tarot, Superintendent . . . There are a number of schools of thought on its origins, perhaps the most popular one of which is that it originated in Italy in the fourteenth-century, another that it came from Ancient Egypt. And as one would expect in circumstances such as these—where there is an absence of indisputable proof as to the true origins—the original individual meanings of the cards, and the way in which to lay them out to read and interpret have become lost over the centuries.

"So what one may find is that in some instances two, shall we say, 'authorities' on the Tarot, will agree on what they believe to be the true meanings of a card or cards, and in other instances, the meanings given by these two authorities would appear to be at complete variance with one another.

"This is where Professor Roxeth and I are in such violent disagreement with each other . . . aside, that is, from the fact that he is of the Egyptian school of thought, while I, not surprisingly, am of the Italian. I would not argue that Professor Roxeth's knowledge of the history of the Tarot is anything other than of the very highest order. Unfortunately, when it comes to interpreting the cards, he is a rank amateur. His interpretations are literal, text-book translations of the meanings of the cards. Anyone can buy a book of instruction on how to use the Tarot, but one *must* have the gift, Superintendent, to be able to look at the cards and *know*, know with the surety of the skilled specialist who reads an X-ray picture, exactly what the shadows, the shades of light and dark mean."

There was a time when David would have impatiently brushed aside such a statement and indeed, had it been made by anyone other than Mrs. Charles, his reaction would have been precisely that, to dismiss what she had said as the pretentious humbug of a quack. Mrs. Charles, he had long since discovered, was not given to self-aggrandisement, neither was she a quack. He didn't pretend to understand her, what made her the way she was but he did believe in her, implicitly.

"We come now," she continued, "to my reason for bringing you out tonight."

Again well to the right of the other cards, she laid down a further card. "*The Sun* . . . inverted, I think," she said slowly, "preceded by—" she hesitated as though she were making up her mind about something, then laid down another card "*—The World*." Her hand lingered for a moment on the second card as if reluctant to relinquish it. She gazed at these, the last two cards, for another moment and then raised her eyes to David's face.

"*The Sar, The Moon, The Sun* . . . Or to quote the old familiar saying," she went on, " '*the sun, the moon and the stars*'. One generally uses that particular adage to convey the sentiment that one has either given or is prepared to give of one's all in some way or another, usually to some other person. *The Star, The Moon* and *The Sun* are cards seventeen, eighteen and nineteen in the Major Arcana, and the Tarot murderer has kept to that, their correct sequence in the Tarot. But reverse the sequence to read *The Sun, The Moon* and *The Star* and those three cards then embody the Tarot murderer. With these cards he tells the world that he has given his all."

"You're saying that the Tarot murderer is definitely not yet through with his fun and games? There's going to be a third, a *final* Tarot vistim?"

"I fear that that is correct, Superintendent. His third victim might've already received the first card, *The World,* in which case we are probably too late. However, there was a pause of five weeks between the first two Tarot murders, and hopefully there will be a similar time lapse between the second murder and the third. It is not yet three weeks since Lorna Lock was murdered, so there is some hope that we will be in time."

"Are you telling me that you think the Tarot murderer gives some warning to his victim before he strikes by sending her a card from the Tarot?" He glanced at those lying on the table. "In Miriam Noad's case, *The Tower of Destruction,* and in Lorna Lock's, *Justice?"*

"I don't think, Superintendent, I *know* that in both instances, the card left by the Tarot murderer with his victim was preceded by another card. Lorna Lock, when she came to see me shortly before she was murdered, told me that she had received a card from the Tarot *(Justice)*; and I have very good reason to believe that she took that card to Rupert Roxeth for him to interpret. You are aware, are you not, that Amery Walters trains horses for Professor Roxeth and that Peter Walters and the Sutherlands' godson are on fairly intimate terms with him, as was Lorna Lock, according to John? And also that it is for Rupert Roxeth and certain archaeological aspirations of his associated with his interest in the Tarot that John—and Peter—are supposedly prepared to give up their university studies?"

"No," said David, slightly taken aback. "At least, I know that Roxeth has horses with Walters, but this is the first I've heard of John's personal association with the man. I wonder if James and Mary know—?"

"I should imagine so . . . Before I proceed with any new venture—take on a new client—this is the first question I ask myself. Motive . . . *why* has that person come to me. Seldom is it for the reason or reasons given. There is always a grain of truth in what I'm told, but usually the problem turns out to be far more complex than that which has been laid before me. Mr. and Mrs. Sutherland's motives for asking you to approach me about the Tarot murders didn't ring quite as true as I should have liked. And yet it was as I would have expected. . . ."

"You think that James and Mary know about John's involvement with Roxeth and that they hoped you'd unmask the fellow as some kind of charlatan—I suppose," he added with a shrug, "in the hope that John would see the light of day before it was too late."

"That would appear to be the most logical assumption. However, their fears are quite groundless. In confidence, John has confessed to me that he has always had every intention of returning to college and that he's been obliged to indulge in this deception on his friend's behalf. Peter Walters is apparently much taken with the good professor. And so, it would seem, was Lorna Lock."

"If, as you've said, Lorna went to Roxeth with a Tarot card, why didn't he mention that fact to the police?"

"There could be many reasons— We must avoid the temptation to speculate . . . it will only confuse matters. Though I must confess that this is one of the reasons why I had hoped to delay contacting you for a little while longer. I wanted to feel more sure of myself. I don't like jumping to conclusions about anyone, and I'm especially cautious when someone for whom I have so little regard is involved. It's all too easy to let one's prejudices cloud the issue."

Yes, thought David, that was true enough. Hadn't petty prejudice once blinded him to the truth and predisposed him to hang the murderer's label round her neck?

"What did Roxeth tell the girl?" he asked. "Did she say?"

"It was all very garbled . . . She was greatly distressed, and I am therefore reluctant to place too much emphasis on what little she did have to say about the Professor and his interpretation of *Justice*. She was, however, quite convinced that that card was her death warrant."

"You wouldn't agree with that interpretation?"

"Most definitely I wouldn't. And yet it *was* her death warrant. It isn't the card that I, were I the Tarot murderer, would've elected to send to her as a forewarning of what was to come . . . that's if the composite picture which I've built up of him and his motives is accurate. One therefore forms a very definite impression of the Tarot murderer. He is an amateur."

David could not resist a smile. "In other words, he doesn't have the gift."

"No, Superintendent," she said decisively, "he does *not* have the gift. We are dealing with someone who likes to play games, a person who cares nothing for human life and thinks himself a very clever fellow indeed. And there we have his one big weakness. I have no doubt that the Tarot murderer, whoever that person is, knows of my interest in him, and he won't be able to resist the temptation, he will have to show off, prove to everyone that he is indeed the clever fellow that he thinks himself. Our hope lies in his assessment of me as compared with his opinion of himself, which of us he thinks is the smarter. From the impression I have thus far formed of him, there will be, in his opinion, no contest. And that is what we must aim for. The Tarot murderer must be encouraged to think of me as the complete fool."

The clairvoyante paused and seemed for the moment to be lost in thought. Then she went on:

"We must now apply ourselves to the prevention of the third Tarot murder. And in the furtherance of that aim, I need your help to find someone for me. A drifter, a down-and-out known to the social workers at The Good Samaritan in Gidding as 'Scottie'."

David's eyebrows shot right up. "Scottie the sculptor?"

"You know the gentleman?"

"Everyone does— He's quite a well-known character round Gidding, certainly with the police while I was with them. We used to see a lot of him before Povey— the chap from St. Luke's—got The Good Samaritan on the go. Scottie sleeps it off there now instead of in the cells. Talented fellow."

"Do you think you could arrange to have him traced?"

"That should be no problem. Povey's bound to know where he is."

"I've been told that Scottie hasn't been seen at The Good Samaritan for some time. He's thought to be somewhere on the road back home to Scotland."

He nodded. "Leave it with me. I'll see what I can do. How do you expect him to help you with your enquiries?" he asked with the ghost of a smile.

"I think he knows, possibly unwittingly, who the Tarot murderer is. I've reason to believe that in the same way Lorna Lock approached Professor Roxeth and me about the card which she'd been sent by the Tarot murderer, Miriam Noad went to Scottie. I understand that he's quite a knowledgeable gentleman, well-informed, and as I've said, I think Miriam Noad asked him if he knew anything about the Tarot and what *The Tower of Destruction*—the card the Tarot murderer had sent her—meant."

"That rather makes finding him top priority, doesn't it?"

"If the Tarot murderer is in a position where he can observe my every move, then I cannot stress strongly enough how urgent it is that Scottie is found as quickly as possible. Once the Tarot murderer discovers that I know about this man—"

David finshed the sentence for her. "Scottie the sculptor becomes a threat to him." He rose. "I'll get on to it first thing in the morning."

"There was one other thing, Superintendent," she said slowly. "I want you to arrange something for me."

He smiled to himself. This had started out as a simple request for a reading of two cards from the Tarot and now . . . "Something *à la* the Stuart necklace?" he enquired, recalling their collaboration on the unmasking of another murderer.

"In a way, yes. A fete is to be held on Saturday in the grounds of the Gidding General Hospital. At this fete a young woman is to be crowned Miss Gidding General in recognition of certain fund raising activities in which she and a number of other girls have been involved during the year. It is imperative that I read the Tarot for that girl. At this function, if possible."

"Good lord!" he exclaimed. "You don't believe in doing things by halves, do you? How on earth do you think I'll be able to fix that?"

"Oh, I'm sure you'll find a way, Superintendent," she assured him sweetly. "Once you apply your mind to it."

"I did that small job for them late last year," he

said meditatively. "Spate of petty pilfering. The company which employs me as their chief security adviser, was called in to do something about the matter and I was sent along to the hospital to give my views . . . came up with a couple of ideas which seemed to please the powers that be—" He paused reflectively. "Which reminds me . . . I had a letter of thanks from the hospital afterwards and Roxeth's name was one of those listed on the letter-heading. It's an unusual name and it struck a chord when I heard it mentioned again in connection with the Tarot murders."

Mrs. Charles smiled at the thoughtful expression on his face. "We must not be too hasty in our condemnation of the poor man," she warned him.

"No," he sighed. "All the same, I must say that I'm beginning to feel increasingly uneasy about our learned friend. They tell me he's got something of a shady past, too. Goes back to the time he was a don at one of the universities. Bit of a fuss about him and one of the girl students."

He looked at Mrs. Charles as if he expected her to know all about the incident, but the closed expression on her face disclosed nothing either way.

"I must also say," he went on after a moment, "that I have the greatest respect and admiration for you, Madame. You are the most charitable person I have ever met."

"Thank you for the compliment, Superintendent," she responded gravely. "And thank heaven that you cannot read my thoughts for then you would have nowhere near so high a regard for me."

He smiled. Then he said, "Well, I'll do my best about Scottie and can make no promises about the fete. Your victim, Miss Gidding General . . . Who is she?"

"A rather beautiful young creature by the name of Karen Wheeler."

"Miriam Noad's flat-mate?"

"And runner-up in the Miss Gidding General contest."

"Since when does the runner-up get to wear the winner's crown?"

"When something unfortunate happens to that person, the winner. Like murder, Superintendent," she said quietly.

Fusion of Ideas

The inquest on Lorna Lock was held the following morning.

"Interesting," remarked David Sayer afterwards as he escorted Mrs. Charles into Alice's Tea-rooms, "what the pathologist had to say about some of the bruises on the back of the girl's neck . . . that the bruising could have occurred some while before she died."

Mrs. Charles considered the claim that Old Jack, the stable-hand who had caught Lorna snooping around Amery Walters' horse-boxes several hours before she was murdered, had made concerning the bruising on her neck, but made no comment.

It was reasonably quiet in the tea-rooms but they nevertheless selected a secluded corner where none of their conversation was likely to be overheard.

They remained silent until the waitress had brought them their tea, and then Mrs. Charles said, "Well, Superintendent: you have some news for me, I hope."

"Bad news, I'm afraid," he said.

"Scottie the sculptor," she guessed, sighing, "is dead."

"Yes . . . Cause of death hasn't yet been established, but foul-play is a distinct possibility. The Gidding lads are wondering if our friend has struck again. The poor wretch had a Tarot card on him. *The Tower of Destruction*." He paused and shook his head reproachfully. "You do get me into some dodgy situations . . . It was as well that I took the precaution of having a word with Povey down at The Good Samaritan about Scottie and his whereabouts and that Povey more or less requested me to make an official enquiry on his behalf, otherwise I would've had some very fast explaining to do. The police are funny about little things like strange coincidences, you know. They take a very dim view of them."

Mrs. Charles' eyes twinkled at him. "Why, Superintendent! you're becoming quite devious."

"Yes," he said grimly. "Old habits die hard, but I'm learning. It hurts me as an ex-police officer to admit it, but there are occasions when your way of doing things would appear to have its merits. And anyway, feeling as I do right now about friend Roxeth, I wouldn't want to tip him our hand . . . have him get to hear how much you've discovered about the Tarot murderer."

"When and where was Scottie's body found?"

"A couple of hitch-hikers stumbled across it late yesterday afternoon on the road North. About eight miles out on the other side of Gidding. Concealed in a ditch. Head bashed in, possibly from a fall after a heavy drinking session. He'd been dead for some time."

"A day, a week?" she probed.

"Something like six or seven weeks, the doctor said." His eyes narrowed. "Why? What are you thinking?"

"You don't find anything significant about that— that the man whom I believe to have been Miriam Noad's confidant over the card that the Tarot murderer sent her, should meet with an unfortunate accident and die only a short while, perhaps less than a week, after the Tarot murderer had struck for the first time?"

"You think Scottie was another of his victims."

"Yes, I do, Superintendent. But not in the same way that Miriam Noad and Lorna Lock were. The Tarot murderer couldn't risk going after his second victim, Lorna Lock, until he'd got Scottie out of the way. I am now more than ever convinced that Scottie knew who the Tarot murderer is: either because Miriam Noad suspected that she knew the identity of the person who had sent her *The Tower of Destruction* and confided that person's name in Scottie; or because that person was, *is*, someone from The Good Samaritan who knew that Scottie, a man of quite good intellect, might put two and two together and make an intelligent guess as to who the Tarot murderer is."

He nodded slowly. Then, after a moment or two, he grinned slyly and said, "It's going to be interesting to hear what Roxeth makes of the card that was found on Scottie . . . assuming that after the police get the pathologist's report on Scottie, his death is treated as another Tarot murder and Roxeth is called in again. We, you and I, know that the Tarot murderer didn't leave any card with Scottie." He chuckled. "Someone is going to look an absolute fool when it all comes out . . . providing," he added, raising his eyebrows a fraction, "that you do get to the bottom of these murders."

There was a far away expression in Mrs. Charles' eyes. "A fool . . . Professor Roxeth?" She seemed puzzled by the allusion. Then, frowning: "*Vingt-deux* . . . Do you know what that means, Superintendent?"

He shook his head. "It sounds French."

"It is. The French for twenty-two." She looked dismayed. "Professor Roxeth isn't the fool. I am beginning to wonder if it isn't Adele Herrmann."

"Pardon, Madame?" he said.

She shook her head quickly. "You must forgive me, Superintendent. I am letting my thoughts stray. Now, let us get back to the matter of Saturday's fete. Have you anything for me there?"

"Yes, I think we are in luck. As I was driving home last night, I suddenly remembered that Mary Sutherland does a great deal of charity work for various good causes in and around Gidding, so I had a word with her over the phone this morning and she seems to think that she can help us. She knows Lady Felton— the fete organiser—quite well. Mary, of course, wanted to know what we are up to . . . I had to tell her something."

"Yes?" she said expectantly.

"I said you anticipated that the Tarot murderer would be at the fete and that you were of the opinion that if he knew you were there, too, he wouldn't be able to resist the temptation to show how much cleverer he is than anyone else—*you*—by asking you to read the Tarot for him."

"Mrs. Sutherland was satisfied with that explanation?"

"I think so. As for the girl, Miss Gidding General— That's going to be tricky: I'm still working on it. But rest assured that Mary's got no idea that you're harbouring such nasty evil suspicions about the girl's sudden rise to fame."

Mrs. Charles was gazing past him out of the window at an attractive, dark-haired young woman who was waiting at the pelican crossing near the entrance to Alice's Tea-rooms.

"I wonder," she said abruptly, averting her gaze so that she was now looking directly at David, "if you would excuse me, Superintendent?" She had gathered up her handbag and was already hurrying towards the door to the street. "I have just seen someone I would like to have a few words with while I have the opportunity. . . ."

Thoughtfully, David watched the clairvoyante move swiftly over the pedestrian crossing and then stop a young woman on the other side of the road.

"Now what's she up to?" he asked himself as Mrs. Charles and Lorna Lock's older sister, Veronica, disappeared into the flower gardens beyond the public lending library.

Mrs. Charles and Veronica Lock found an empty bench in a shady corner of the gardens and sat down.

The clairvoyante began by explaining who she was and confessing to the girl that her sister Lorna had come to see her shortly before she was murdered. "Aside from Lorna's murderer," Mrs. Charles went on, "I strongly suspect that I was the last person to see your sister alive. I make this admission to you in the strictest confidence. There are only five people who either know or knew that Lorna came to see me that night. Lorna, an ex-superintendent of police on whose behalf I have undertaken to interpret the meanings of the cards connected with the Tarot murders—myself, of course—Professor Roxeth and last but by no means least, the Tarot murderer himself."

"You're working with the police?"

"No. They know nothing of my involvement with your sister."

Veronica's grey eyes took on a look of distrust. "But—" She hesitated. "Mr. *(Professor?)* Roxeth gave evidence at the inquest this morning: if he knows that Lorna went to see you, he would've surely told the police about it."

"Not necessarily, my dear. Professor Roxeth may have some very definite reasons of his own for not making that fact known to the police."

"You think—?" The girl paused. Then, reflectively: "Lorna spoke once of a professor . . . I thought she meant one of her university professors. He gave a party—this was some time last Christmas—and she went to it." Veronica spoke haltingly and looked confused. "Professor Roxeth lives somewhere near here?" she enquired.

"He lives on the late Lord Camberley's estate just outside Gidding."

The girl nodded. "Then it's probably the same professor. Lorna promised Daddy and me that she'd spend Christmas with us, then at the last minute, which was typical of her, she disappeared. When she finally reappeared, I asked her where she'd been and she just laughed and said that she'd changed her mind about spending Christmas at home and had gone to a party at the Professor's house instead . . . Somewhere in the country was all that I could get her to tell me about where she'd been."

And Amery Walters' secretary, the resolute Miss Braithwaite, Mrs. Charles recalled fleetingly, had spoken of Lorna making a nuisance of herself over Christmas. . . .

"What would you suppose was the big attraction for Lorna in Gidding?" asked the clairvoyante reflectingly.

Veronica thought for a minute. "Well, in view of what you've just told me, it could've been Mr., I mean, *Professor* Roxeth. But when she pleaded with Daddy to use his influence to get her a job with Mr. Walters, I began to wonder if— Well," she said, frowning, "it was unusual for Lorna to want anything that badly. She just didn't seem to care about anyone or anything . . . except horses that is. She was always potty about horses. Other kids kept pin-ups of pop stars, but Lorna's bedroom had pictures of horses plastered everywhere. On the walls, in the wardrobe, outside the wardrobe, even pinned to the curtains when she ran out of space everywhere else. Still," she sighed, "there were other people with horses nearer to London to whom she could've gone for work."

"You thought she might've been romantically interested in Peter Walters," said Mrs. Charles matter-of-factly.

"It crossed my mind," the girl admitted. "Especially in view of her recent, extremely erratic behaviour. I'd heard through some mutual friends of ours—Lorna's and mine—that she'd made a dreadful spectacle of him during the term over some play or other that he'd written; and that was so like her . . . to be difficult with anyone she really liked. That's why she and Daddy used to fight so dreadfully whenever they got together. Poor Lorna," she said wistfully. "It was as though the more she loved or liked someone, the harder she worked at destroying all hope of any reciprocal feeling.

"It was very true what Daddy said at the inquest this morning," she went on musingly. "Lorna was never the same after poor Mummy's accident. It was a pity—" She paused, frowning. "I know this sounds a dreadful thing to say, but for Lorna's sake, it was a pity that Mummy wasn't killed outright in the acci-

dent that she and Lorna had. I think that in those
months before she eventually died, having to watch
her sitting there in her wheel-chair, little more than a
vegetable . . . it turned Lorna's brain. You'd think,
with your father a psychiatrist, that he would've been
able to help her, but I don't honestly think that Daddy
could see what was happening to her. You can never
see what's right there under your nose, staring you in
the face, can you? And then it was too late. Lorna
became hell-bent on her own destruction and there
was no stopping her."

"I understand that your mother's name was Lorna,
too, and that after her death, your sister chose to be
known by her middle name."

"Yes, for a little while. Then everyone automatically
reverted to using 'Lorna' again. Most of our friends
and relatives found it to difficult, after having called
her 'Lorna' for almost seventeen years, to remember
to call her by her middle name, 'Maude' . . . Maudie."

"The initial necklet that she was known to have
been wearing on the night she was murdered dated
from that time . . . when she wanted to be called
'Maudie'?"

Veronica gave a short, dry laugh. "Lorna stole
that . . . I can't prove it, of course, but—" She hesitated,
then shrugging: "To put it as nicely as I can, Lorna
was very light-fingered. She never paid for anything,
never even—to the best of my knowledge—carried any
money on her. What she wanted she stole—food, clothing . . . hitch-hiked wherever she went, lived rough
. . ." She frowned. "There was absolutely no need
for it. Daddy has always been more than generous to
both of us. He never . . . well, cut her off, so to speak—

regardless of how much her anti-social behaviour distressed and embarrassed him."

"You say she lived rough . . . Surely not here in Gidding? I understand that she had digs somewhere."

Veronica smiled sadly and then gazed slowly round the parched gardens. "I'd say that this was a likely spot . . . A big cardboard carton tucked away somewhere—over there, perhaps, under those bushes," she said with a wave of an arm in their direction. "That's the kind of digs Lorna went in for. She was arrested once in London for sleeping rough on the pavement in one of those big cornflakes cartons and for behaving in a disorderly fashion when moved on by the police. Daddy had to go down to the police station the next day and bail her out." Her voice caught a little. "I'm happy for her that she's dead. It was the only way she could ever have been at peace with herself." She gazed anxiously into Mrs. Charles' eyes. "That sounds harsh and unkind, but you understand what I mean, don't you?"

"Yes. I think you loved your sister very much."

The girl looked down at her hands and nodded. "We were a very close, happy family until the accident and then . . ." Her voice tailed off into a nostalgic silence.

After a discreet pause, Mrs. Charles asked:

"Would you have any idea when Lorna started to wear the initial necklet?"

She shook her head. "I can only tell you when I first noticed her wearing it. How long she'd had it before that, I don't know . . . though I don't think she had it before Christmas."

"It was *after* Christmas that she suddenly started wearing it?"

"Yes."

"Did you say anything to her about it—ask how she'd come by it?"

"No." The girl shook her head sorrowfully. "She'd only have lied to me, especially as it was stolen . . . at least, that's what I've always thought. If it wasn't stolen from a jeweller's—she often went on shop-lifting sprees, just for the hell of it—then it was stolen from somebody she knew or had met up with somewhere."

"I know you must have been asked this question many many times, but are you absolutely sure that neither you nor your sister knew Miriam Noad?"

"The Tarot murderer's first victim?" Veronica widened her eyes and slowly shook her head. "Not as far as I know. I certainly didn't know her, and I never heard Lorna mention anyone of that name, though I couldn't be positive about it . . . that Lorna didn't know her. Lorna got around a fair bit: there must be a lot of people who knew her that Daddy and I don't know about, people from all walks of life."

"Did Lorna ever mention a man called Scottie? Scottie the sculptor is how he was known to the police."

Veronica was shaking her head.

"Then what about The Good Samaritan? Did she ever mention that name to you?"

Again the girl shook her head. Then she frowned: "Wait a minute. There *was* something . . . When I asked her where she'd been over Christmas, she shrugged and said she'd been playing the good Samaritan and had gone to the Professor's party. I took it—her reference to the good Samaritan—to mean that her attendance at this party had been some kind of sacrifice on her part—as if it were something that she hadn't really wanted to do . . . she'd been obliged to go along to it on someone else's account. It meant something else, did it?"

"Yes," said Mrs. Charles. "I think it's the missing link I've been trying to find—the link between your sister and Miriam Noad."

"You mean they *did* know one another?"

"Yes, my dear: I'm convinced of it . . . and that the initial necklet which your sister started wearing soon after Christmas originally belonged to Miriam Noad."

"Lorna stole it from *her*? Where—at the Professor's party?"

"That," said the clairvoyante, "is something I mean to find out."

XV   THE DEVIL
A Man of Some Influence

Rupert Roxeth must have heard Mrs. Charles and decided to oblige her for his sumptuous Rolls-Royce was waiting outside The Bungalow when she returned from Gidding shortly after lunch.

As she alighted from the bus which stopped only a short distance from her home, she saw the small, monkey-like figure in the back seat of the car lean forward and address the chauffeur, who nodded then got smartly out of the car and walked briskly towards her.

"Good afternoon, ma'am," he greeted her, touching his peaked cap deferentially. "I am Mr. Rupert Roxeth's chauffeur. Mr. Roxeth presents his greetings and apologies for the intrusion, but he wonders if you would be good enough to spare him a few moments of your time. He wishes to speak with you on a matter of some urgency. If you would kindly join him in his car, please ma'am, he would be most obliged."

"I should prefer it," responded Mrs. Charles, "if Professor Roxeth were to join me in my home. If you would be so kind as to convey my invitation to the Professor and say that I welcome the opportunity to talk with him."

The chauffeur touched the peak of his cap and bowed stiffly from the waist. "Thank you, ma'am."

Rupert Roxeth's resemblance to a wizened old monkey, thought Mrs. Charles, was more than ever apparent as he sat hunched over in the big comfortable armchair near the fireplace watching her. There was something almost deformed about him and yet when standing and walking, his small frame was youthfully erect, his movements gracefully agile.

"I am obliged to you, Madame," he began formally. "In view of the regrettable animosity which has existed between us in the past, it was most gracious of you to consent to see me."

"I bear you no ill-will, Professor Roxeth," she assured him evenly.

His eyes narrowed. "But surely, Madame . . . after what happened to Lady Camberley—?"

"There is some reason why I should feel ill-disposed towards you on her account?"

"But Madame," he said, his dark eyes burning into hers, "you were aware, were you not—and can't possibly have forgotten—that it was I, *Tarot,* and not you whom Lady Camberly chose to heed at the time of her proposed marriage to Lord Camberley?"

"No, Professor Roxeth, I've not forgotten. Nor have I forgotten that my prophecy for Lady Camberley, if she chose to disregard my advice, ultimately came to pass."

A dangerous glint showed in Roxeth's eyes. "For which, Madame, I have always held you wholly responsible." He crouched forward in his chair, his head sinking even deeper into his chest. "You *willed* it . . . encouraged Sophia to harbour negative thoughts about her marriage and her life with Camberley. *You deliberately put the idea of suicide into her head.*"

Mrs. Charles regarded him imperturbably. He was a bad man, the kind, she thought, whom one could easily picture having an evil influence over others, anyone who got too close to him. Playing about with another person's life, bending that person's will to his own would be a game to him, a diverting pastime for his own vile amusement. . . .

She raised her eyebrows quizzically. "To what end, Professor Roxeth? To see that sweet young girl suffer as she did, to see you ultimately set up comfortably for life following her husband's demise when it wouldn't have been unreasonable to expect that she would've survived him by a good many years and been able to salvage something of her life before her time eventually came?" She shook her head and smiled coldly. "Thought transference, had it been considered by me, would not have taken the form which you have suggested, I can assure you. If such had been my intention, then I would have used my every endeavour to ensure that Sophia, *not you*, Professor Roxeth, lived happily ever after."

A look of cunning came into Roxeth's eyes. "You admit then that your powers are not what you claim?"

"Powers?" The clairvoyante sounded amused. "I have only the one power and that relates solely to myself, my gift of second sight . . . the power to see that which lies beyond, that which only the seeker, no one else, has the power to change should he or she wish it otherwise. Sophia chose not to heed my advice following my reading of the Tarot for her—for what I've always believed to have been totally selfless reasons. And your contra-advice in no way influenced that decision. Sophia wouldn't have come to me had she not already known in her heart of hearts that the marriage was wrong for her. I merely gave voice and form to her subconscious doubts and fears."

"You're very sure of yourself, Madame," he observed coolly.

"I've never had any time for hypocrisy, Professor Roxeth," she said, a trifle wearily. "I am what I am, blest with an extraordinary gift which to deny would be to demean it."

He smiled crookedly. "On that point, Madame—the degree of excellence of your gift of clairvoyance—I should always beg the right to differ. I, too, you will observe find pretence tiresome . . . But it wasn't to make such an assurance to you that I wished to talk with you today." He paused, his dark eyes fixed on her. "This morning, Madame . . . you were present at the inquest on Lorna Lock. I observed you sitting with Mr. Sayer, a gentleman whom I know to have once been closely associated with the Gidding police. I would ask you, Madame, what your interest is in this affair of the Tarot murders. Do you propose to challenge my interpretation of the Tarot cards? You've quite a reputation in these parts, I understand, following the clearing up of an unsolved murder which took place hereabouts some years ago. I've been led to believe that clairvoyance wasn't used in that instance to unmask the killer, that you used more conventional methods to get to the bottom of the murder, but nevertheless, people being people, they are bound to have greatly romanticised the whole affair and are therefore more than likely to pay quite a good deal of attention to anything you may have to say about the Tarot murders."

"Apparently you're assuming that I'd disagree with your findings."

"You've read the newspapers . . . what I've said about the cards the Tarot murderer left with his victims?"

"I've made it my business to acquaint myself with your comments on the Tarot cards concerned with these murders . . ."

"And?"

She did not answer.

"I see," he said. He put his hands together and made a pyramid with his finger-tips. "You intend to make your views known to the police?"

"That wasn't my intention."

"Then I ask you again, Madame: what is your interest in the Tarot murders?"

She feigned surprise. "But surely you know the answer to that question, Professor Roxeth?" She paused, her expression hardening. "After all, you were the one who advised Lorna Lock against allowing Madame Herrmann to read the Tarot for her."

Like two cats with but the one mouse between them they sat watching one another, each waiting for the other to make that first, possibly fatal, move.

Roxeth's eyes narrowed. "Lorna came to see you? *When?*"

"After she'd received a card taken from the Major Arcana. *Justice . . . The card Lorna told me she'd taken to you to read.*"

There was a long silence. Nothing showed in Roxeth's eyes.

"You would appear, Madame," he said at length, "to have me at something of a disadvantage."

"Yes," she said simply.

"I would deny it, of course . . . if you went to the police and told them what you know. But then, on reflection, perhaps what we have here is not so much of a checkmate situation as a draw. Neither of us can make a move." He smiled thinly. "It occurs to me that the police would be very interested to know that Lorna Lock consulted you about a card from the Tarot, a fact which—and please correct me if I'm wrong—they would appear to know nothing about."

"I have no intention of going to the police about you or anyone else."

"What, Madame, am I to take that to mean?" His eyebrows rose and he eyed her mockingly. "That you know who the Tarot murderer is?"

"Yes, Professor Roxeth. Just that. I know who he is."

The look on Roxeth's face was one of utter disbelief. "You'll forgive my scepticism, Madame, but that isn't possible." His eyes darkened with contempt. "If it had been there in the cards, his identity, *I* would've seen it."

"That, Professor Roxeth, is debatable," she said smoothly. "However, I don't propose to take issue with you in this instance because you happen to be right. The identity of the Tarot murderer wasn't contained in the cards."

"So how then do *you* know who he is?"

"*The Fool* . . . I believe that in your books on the Tarot, you list that card at the beginning of the Major Arcana."

"That is correct. *The Fool* is an unnumbered card, the only one in the Major Arcana, as you know, without a number."

"Yes," she said. "You wouldn't disagree, though, that some—including myself—place *The Fool* on the bottom of the pack, that is to say *after* the other twenty-one cards in the Major Arcana, and give it a number."

"No," he admitted cautiously. "I wouldn't disagree

with you there. I'd consider it to be more the practice of an amateur fortune-teller."

She smiled graciously at the gibe. "And that is how I know who the Tarot murderer is."

A flickering smile on Roxeth's lips widened round a high-pitched, squeaky burst of laughter. Wiping his eyes, he said, "Forgive me, Madame, but one seldom finds anything to amuse one these days: I hesitate not to make the most of so precious a moment. Any number of people place *The Fool* at the end of the Major Arcana," he went on scornfully. "Are you going to accuse *all* of them as being the Tarot murderer?"

A small smile was the clairvoyante's only response to his question.

"You're going to the police with this?"

"I've already told you that that isn't my intention. I do not anticipate that this will be necessary." Mrs. Charles rose. "Now, I regret that I shall have to ask you to excuse me. I'm expecting a caller shortly and I must prepare for his visit."

Roxeth was on his feet in a single, fluid movement.

"There is one question I would like to ask you before you leave," said the clairvoyante. "The Tarot murderer's first victim, Miriam Noad . . . Did you know her?"

"No," he said.

"She didn't attend the party you gave last Christmas for the young people who help out at The Good Samaritan?"

Roxeth's face was impassive, but there was a hint of menace in his tone.

"You've discovered a very great deal in a very short time, Madame . . . Indeed so much that one is moved to wonder that you're not becoming just a little anxious over your present position. You don't fear the Tarot murderer?"

"No," she replied calmly. "Nor any threat that you may make to me."

"You are either very brave, Madame, or recklessly foolish. Were I you, with the knowledge that you claim to have, I should be feeling most insecure. Afraid even."

"There's no need for me to fear someone who doesn't fear me. The Tarot murderer will only become a threat to me if that situation should alter."

Roxeth gave her a long, hard look. Then he bowed a little and said, "I am obliged to you, Madame." He crossed to the door, then paused and looked back at her. There was a small, mocking smile on his lips.

"The first I knew of Miriam Noad," he said evenly, "was when I, a recognised authority on the Tarot, was approached by the Gidding police to assist them with their enquiries into her murder. I didn't know the young woman personally. But," he went on, the mocking smile still very much in evidence in his eyes, "that isn't to say that she wasn't amongst the three hundred or so guests who attended the party to which you referred. She might've been there at some time during the evening, come and gone again as many young people did that night, without my ever having been aware of her presence. Then again, in view of the fact that she was a nurse, it's more than likely that she was on duty at the hospital that night. The invitation to the handful of young people who assist Theodore Povey with his work at The Good Samaritan was a general one. Nobody received a specific invitation. I do not give that kind of party. . . ."

* * *

Mrs. Charles remained quietly in the room for some minutes listening to Rupert Roxeth's Rolls-Royce attain the higher reaches of the access road to the motorway, and thinking about the night that Lorna Lock had come banging on her door. She had a good ear for sound which made comparison relatively easy. It wasn't with Rupert Roxeth that Lorna Lock had hitched a lift that night. . . .

XVI   THE TOWER OF DESTRUCTION
(or THE LIGHTNING STRUCK TOWER)
The Beginning of the End

The Reverend Theodore Povey was an exceptionally tall man, just beginning to show signs of going grey, thin, bespectacled, and with such an overall weak countenance that most people, on meeting him for the first time, were convinced that there must be two Theodore Poveys and that this was not *the* Theodore Povey, the human dynamo behind The Good Samaritan.

As arranged by his wife with Mrs. Charles, who had telephoned while he was out that morning, he arrived at The Bungalow at two thirty prompt, and after conveying greetings from the Vicar of St. Stephen's, whom he had been visiting in the village, he smilingly expressed his curiosity over her desire to see him.

"My wife," he then went on, "inferred that it was on a matter of the utmost urgency."

"The Tarot murders," explained Mrs. Charles.

"Ah," he said, his neat, rather feminine eyebrows arched expressively over his rimless glasses. "You're quite a celebrity in Gidding, Madame: I'm not unfamiliar with your name and your professional activities, and can naturally understand your interest in these terrible crimes; but I'm puzzled that you should wish to talk to me about them. While, admittedly, I was quite well-acquainted with Miriam Noad, I know no more of her murder, or of the one subsequent to it, than what I've read in the newspapers and viewed on television."

"No," she said gravely. "You know a great deal

more about them than that. Indirectly, these crimes
had their beginnings with you."

"Really, Madame!" Reverend Povey's eyebrows shot
up emphasising the indignation in his voice. "I can't
begin to think how."

"With The Good Samaritan, Mr. Povey. Somewhere
around Christmas of last year."

This time Theodore Povey was silent.

"You're not surprised, I think," she observed.

"The large cross-section of people we get at The
Good Samaritan makes anything possible, Madame,"
he said archly. "And, of course, as one of our helpers,
Miriam Noad came into very close contact with these
people. I sincerely hope that I'm mistaken in thinking
that you're suggesting that one of them is responsible
for Miriam's death. That would be intolerable. I can't
bear even to think of it! Miriam was a dedicated, true
Christian . . . in every sense of the word. It's unthink-
able that someone whom she helped back along the
road of life repaid the debt he owed her by taking
her life. She was the most popular girl down at the
Centre, both with the helpers and with the helped."

"So I understand," said Mrs. Charles. "But I wonder
if you'd be kind enough to cast your mind back to last
Christmas. Was Miriam involved in any unpleasantness at The Good Samaritan, either with another
member of your staff or with any of those who come
to you for help?"

He looked at her wonderingly and shook his head.

"It might've been something quite trivial, seemingly
unimportant to you. . . ."

"Well, there was one thing," he admitted hesitantly.
"But as you've said, it was really quite a trifling matter, and it was more or less cleared up, anyway. Miriam

mislaid some jewellery—one of these initial necklets that seem to be all the rage with young people at the moment—but it turned out that the theft had occurred at the hospital where she worked."

"Miriam got her necklet back?"

"No, I don't believe so. As a matter of fact, in a way it was all rather a bit strange. I didn't quite know what to make of it at the time, and then when I spoke to Karen—Miriam's best friend—about it, Karen said that Scottie (one of our lost sheep) had been drinking all morning and had got it all wrong, and that the necklet had been stolen from Miriam at the hospital."

"What did Scottie tell you about Miriam and her necklet?"

"Scottie is one of our more regular regulars, if you know what I mean. Poor fellow . . . seldom sober . . . knows he's not allowed to consume any alcohol on the premises—we accept people for what they are, but nevertheless, we simply cannot permit drug-taking and drinking within the four walls of The Good Samaritan," he said severely. "I wasn't there on this particular morning—it was a Sunday. I only know from Karen what really went on. But apparently it was fairly quiet . . . Miriam and Karen were the only two helpers there, and Scottie somehow smuggled in some liquor, then tucked himself away in a corner of one of the little-used rooms and quietly got on with a heavy drinking session.

"Now, according to Scottie's version of what happened that morning, while he was in this room, Miriam and another girl came in and had a fight . . . Y'know, fisticuffs!" The pretty eyebrows shot up. "No holds barred! Scottie said that without knowing that he was there, Miriam came into the room to collect her things to go home—it was the room where the staff usually left their belongings—and then this other girl came in and they started to fight. Scottie said the other girl ripped the necklet from around Mirian's neck and screamed out something like, '*That's mine, give it to me!*', and then she stormed out."

"Did he see who this girl was?"

"No— He only saw the back of her. There's no window or electric light in the room—it used to be a coldstore. The only light came from the passage beyond the room. He said she—the other girl—was wearing jeans and a pullover, but so was Miriam. It's more or less standard uniform. We all wear much the same thing—even I rarely wear anything else when I'm down there. It does away with this 'us and them' barrier. Unless you were personally involved with the work there, you wouldn't know on which side of the fence any of us stand."

"You mentioned the incident to Miriam?"

"Yes. But she just looked surprised and said yes, she'd mislaid her necklet somewhere, but as for there having been a fight, no . . . Scottie must've been imagining things! More or less exactly what Karen told me."

"In view of what you said a moment ago, you obviously still had some doubts about the truth of the matter to have questioned Karen about it."

"Only because Miriam seemed rather upset when I brought the subject up."

"And Karen said the necklet had gone missing at the hospital?"

"She was a bit offhand about it, but her explanation seemed perfectly reasonable to me. I'd heard rumours about other people's personal belongings growing legs and walking out of the hospital, so I was quite happy to leave it at that."

"Do you know where Miriam got the necklet from in the first place?"

"Not for sure. I suspected, though, that one of her hospital patients had given it to her."

"Was there some special reason for your thinking that?"

"Well, to be honest with you, it was Karen who put that idea into my head. Miriam was very depressed (this would've been a week or so before Christmas), moody and irritable, which wasn't at all like her. I asked her if there were anything the matter—if there were something I could do to help—and she said it was nothing . . . it was the end of the year and she was tired—and disappointed that she wasn't going to get a few days' break from the hospital so that she could go home to her parents for a rest.

"Quite frankly, it simply didn't ring true. She was tireless, an indefatigable worker. So I naturally mentioned the matter to Karen. And Karen . . . well, she was rather cryptic about, and I naturally interpreted her remarks as seemed most logical to me. Karen said that Miriam had finally made the cardinal mistake of getting involved, which I took to mean an emotional entanglement, though not necessarily a romantic attachment, to one of her patients . . . one who was unfortunately terminally ill and therefore beyond Miriam's help. Then, soon afterwards, Miriam turned up wearing the initial necklet and I simply put two and two together, no doubt incorrectly, and assumed that her gravely ill patient had given it to her as a Christmas gift."

"A romantic attachment would've been unlikely?"

He smiled solemnly. "Miriam had only one true love and that was nursing, helping others, for which she had an almost divine vocation. She was a jolly girl—always ready for a laugh and some fun—and she enjoyed the company of young men of her own age group. However, in my opinion, she'd never have been unfaithful to her calling. She wasn't a noticeably deeply religious girl, but I think she felt with every fibre in her body that she'd been specially chosen for her kind of work. Which must've been very frustrating for those who fell under her spell—and I think that that would've been most of the young men who either worked with her, or were helped by her, at The Good Samaritan. Even poor old Scottie," he sighed, "was more than half in love with her."

"About Scottie," said Mrs. Charles quietly. "I regret that I have some rather sad news for you. . . ."

The tiny, prefabricated fortune-telling booth provided
for Mrs. Charles at Gidding General Hospital's Summer Garden Fete was neither to her liking nor to her
taste; however, everyone else seemed highly delighted
with it and so her own personal views of its gaily
striped pink and green awning and the bizarre star-
spangled sky-blue walls were kept discreetly to herself.

"They've done a wonderful job," enthused Mary
Sutherland, a petite fifty-four-year-old woman with
pointed, bird-like features. She gazed rapturously at
the amazing spectacle. "In such a short time, too."
She bestowed a glowing smile on Mrs. Charles. "It's
just what I imagined a *proper* fortune-telling booth
would look like."

The clairvoyante took another long, thoughtful look
at the small structure and then, raising her eyebrows,
said, simply, "Is it really?"

Something about her tone made Mary wonder a
little. "You're not happy with it?" she asked anxiously.

"I'm quite delighted with it," Mrs. Charles hastened
to assure her. "I'm extremely grateful to you for your
help: you've been most kind."

"No," said Mary quickly. "I'm the one who's grateful . . . I've felt ever so much better since I've known
that you were willing to help. I *know* everything will
be all right now. I can feel it in my bones."

Mrs. Charles studied her for a moment and then
said, "Shall we inspect the interior now?"

She held her breath as she parted the blue and white

shredded plastic curtain and entered the booth, but her fears were groundless. There wasn't a star or a spangle to be seen anywhere. The inside walls had been painted a sober matt black, which, thought Mrs. Charles wryly, should look well with the gold kaftan that she would change into later. A small, baize-covered table and two chairs had been placed in the centre of the booth.

"Excellent," murmured Mrs. Charles approvingly.

Mary beamed with pleasure, turning quickly and warmly greeting an elderly, grey-haired woman who suddenly exploded through the middle of the curtain. Looking back at Mrs. Charles, Mary then said, "Mrs. Charles—I mean, Madame Herrmann—I should like you to meet the fete's organiser, Lady Felton."

Lady Agnes Felton was built on the lines of an Eastern Bloc woman athlete. She shook Mrs. Charles' hand with gusto and boomed how good it was of Madame Herrmann to donate her time to the charity.

"We thought," Her Ladyship went on, without pausing for breath, "that in view of your reputation, Madame, fifty pence for a ten minute session would not be out of order."

The clairvoyante assented with a small nod of her head and concealed her quiet amusement behind a very grave countenance. In normal circumstances, fifty pence would buy barely a minute of Madame Adele Herrmann's time. But these, she reminded herself, were far from normal circumstances, and one had therefore to be prepared for the odd concession or two here and there.

"Miss Arnold has volunteered to take the money at the door, so to speak," said Lady Felton. "She should be along at any moment now." She smiled happily at the other two women. "Well, must be off—there are a million and one things still to be seen to and . . . good grief! is that the time already? I must fly! Have a good day, ladies."

With a bound, Her Ladyship disappeared through the curtain.

"Quite a character, isn't she?" observed Mary. "Puts everything she's got into this charity work of hers. She used to be a rower. Not quite Olympic standard, but still pretty good."

"I can quite believe it," said Mrs. Charles with a twinkle in her eye.

"Now about Miss Gidding General . . ." said Mary. "She'll be crowned, or sashed—whatever it is that they're going to do to her—immediately after the official opening by the Mayor. Then while the newspaper reporters are still here, we—that is, Lady Felton —thought it would be a good idea from the publicity angle to have Miss Gidding General come straight here to have her fortune told by you. I mean, it *is* something a bit different, isn't it? These things get so hackneyed . . . one is always on the lookout for a fresh approach." She raised her eyebrows at the somewhat surprised expression on Mrs. Charles' face. "You're not happy with that idea?"

"No, no, my dear, it's a perfectly splendid arrangement. It's just that I made a similar suggestion to David Sayer and I naturally expected that he would've said something to you about it."

Mary shook her head. "It must've slipped his memory. But no matter. Great minds think alike, they say— or something very similar. It's all worked out in the end." She gazed round the booth. "Well, I'll leave you to get on with whatever it is that you do. Miss Arnold shouldn't be long. Just give a shout if there's anything you need . . ." She parted the curtain, then paused and said, "By the way, I'll be along sometime today to see you. In your professional capacity, of course," she added with a smile.

"No, my dear— By all means make your donation to Miss Arnold for my time, but I'd prefer that you call on me at my home where I can do justice to a reading of the Tarot for you. This is neither the time nor the place. . . ."

Mary frowned. "Yes, you're quite right. It would be silly of me to take up your time today when I can see you later." She released her grip on the curtain, her frown deepening. "Talking about donations, I don't suppose you'd accept a small bribe?"

Mrs. Charles smiled. "To do what, my dear?"

"Well, I'm not sure, but I think John will be at the fete later on today with some of his friends. If I can inveigle him in here, I don't suppose you'd steer him back to university for James and me?"

"You think he'd listen to me?"

"Probably not," sighed Mary. "But I thought I'd ask. Not a very good idea, though . . . the moment you started talking about going back to university, John would suspect collusion, even if there wasn't any."

"Very probably . . . Young people have a particularly sensitive ear for humbug."

With a rueful smile, Mary turned aside and went through the curtain.

Unhurriedly, Mrs. Charles unpacked her gold silk kaftan from the small suitcase which she had brought with her and changed out of her street clothes. Then, sitting up to the table, she refreshed her make-up and tidied her softly upswept hair.

Ten minutes later, when David Sayer knocked on one of the outer walls of the booth and was bidden to enter, he found her sitting composedly at the table which was now bare except for a pack of Tarot cards.

"Good heavens!" he exclaimed. "I thought for a moment that it was a moon goddess sitting there."

She smiled faintly. "Why *moon*, Superintendent?"

"I don't know," he confessed. "Quite wrong, really. The moon sheds a silvery light, not gold. It was just the first thought that entered my head when I saw you all in gold. Why do you smile?" he asked.

"It's simply that it was such a curious observation for you to make . . . in the circumstances. When one is speaking of the card from the Tarot, *The Moon* in the abstractive means illusion. On a more practical plane it can mean denouncement. It's not a good card, Superintendent."

He gave her a searching look. "I've offended you?"

"Not at all. It just seemed too apt . . . That you should see me correspondingly with the moon—illusion and denouncement with a dash of deception for good measure."

"You expect something of that nature today, a denouncement?"

"It very much depends on whether or not there's been any alteration to the *status quo*. If the Tarot murderer still has no fear of me, then—"

"Will you step into my parlour said the spider to the fly?"

"Something like that . . ." She waved a hand in the air. "What do you think of it, my web?"

"Well," he said cautiously.

"Yes, precisely," she said briskly. "Never mind. All done with the very best of intentions, I'm sure."

"About Karen Wheeler, Miss Gidding General," he began hesitantly. "I haven't yet worked out a way—"

"It's all been taken care of, Superintendent," she interrupted him.

"That's a relief," he admitted. "I was reluctant to tell Mary too much about what you're up to . . . you know, that you're concerned about certain aspects of the girl's friendship with Miriam Noad. Mary wouldn't have let it rest at that: she would've wanted to know why and so on and so forth, and doubtless wouldn't have been able to keep any of it to herself. Lady Kung Fu—or whatever her name is . . . the all-in wrestler!—would've probably got to hear all about it, and the odds are that it would've become common knowledge . . . everyone here today would've known what you were up to, including Karen Wheeler and the Tarot murderer."

"I shouldn't concern yourself too much about the Tarot murderer . . . There'll be no speculation or surprise in that quarter. I very much suspect that he'll find my activities here today highly entertaining and not for one moment be in any doubt as to their true purpose."

He raised his eyebrows and regarded her thoughtfully. Then, after a small pause, he said, "Well, I suppose I'd better let you get on with it. People are starting to roll up now. Looks like they'll get a good crowd. Er . . . by the way. My wife says she's going to pop in and see you a bit later . . . in one of your slack periods," he explained with a sheepish grin. "She's got this idea in mind of dragging me off to the Costa Brava for our holidays this year. Don't know which I hate more—flying or Spanish food! If you'd . . . well, you know—the odd word or two to put her off!"

"Really, Superintendent!"

He gave her another sheepish grin. "Can't blame a desperate man for trying!"

A small, pink pixie-like face framed in masses of fluffy steel-grey hair was suddenly thrust through the curtain. "Irene Arnold," the pixie introduced herself cheerily. "Sorry to interrupt, but it looks like we've got our first customer."

"I'll see you later," David whispered quickly to Mrs. Charles. He nodded to Miss Arnold and then slipped quietly away through the curtain.

"Shall I wheel them in, Madame?" enquired Miss Arnold.

"Them?"

"Well, er, yes: it's a family. They wanted their fortunes told as a family unit so I agreed a special concession . . ."

The clairvoyante's eyebrows rose. This was, she thought, going to be a most interesting day. She only hoped she had the stamina to see it through!

"Before you do that, Miss Arnold . . . show them in . . . I wonder if I might ask for your co-operation on one small matter?"

Mrs. Charles' eyes widened with disbelief as the rest

of Irene Arnold emerged through the curtain. The latter did a quick pirouette and then drew out the voluminous folds of the long black cotton gown she was wearing as if she were a bat in full flight.

"I suddenly remembered that I had this costume up in the attic— I wore it in an amateur theatrical production of *Macbeth*. I was one of the witches," she explained unnecessarily. "I thought it would be most appropriate for today . . . To lend a sense of atmosphere to the occasion. Wouldn't you agree?"

Miss Arnold's eyes shone with enthusiasm and she was generally so very obviously happy and pleased with herself that Mrs. Charles hadn't the heart to disillusion her in any way. Everyone's enthusiasm for her participation in the fete was markedly over-zealous but extremely flattering and kind, and one therefore felt obliged to make exceptions for what, as far as she herself was concerned, was a totally misdirected concept of clairvoyance.

"As you've said, Miss Arnold," she responded, smiling kindly. "Most appropriate. Thank you for taking so much trouble on my account."

Miss Arnold's face lit up with pleasure.

"Now," the clairovyante continued, "we mustn't keep our customers waiting. But first, this little matter I mentioned. In a moment or two, I shall describe someone to you. I anticipate that we'll see quite a lot of people today, but I don't think you'll have too much difficulty with identification. And if, at any time, you've any doubts whatsoever, then I'd like you to react positively—as if you were completely sure of yourself—and follow out my instructions. I don't mind how many false alarms there might be. . . ."

Miss Arnold's head bobbed quickly up and down. "I understand," she said.

"Very well, then. Now, the moment this person passes through the curtain to see me—and I don't want you to act until that time . . . this is *most* important—I want you to close down the booth and then you're to go and fetch the gentleman you saw with me a few minutes ago."

"Mr. Sayer?"

"Good. You know him."

"What if I can't find him?" asked Miss Arnold anxiously.

"You're not to concern yourself. Simply return to the booth and carry on as normal. Mr. and Mrs. Sayer will, no doubt, be popping in to see me at odd intervals during the day, so I think it more than likely that Mr. Sayer will always be somewhere about the place, close at hand."

"Just *Mr.* Sayer?"

"Yes. And that, too, is most important."

Miss Arnold gave a brisk nod. "I've got all that . . . I'll tell anyone who's waiting—that's when I close down—that you're taking a half-hour break after you've seen the person who's just gone in."

"Excellent," said Mrs. Charles. "I know I can rely on you."

"May I ask why—what this is all about?"

"Certainly you may . . . It's a private game that Mr. Sayer and I and this other person are playing between ourselves."

"Somebody's trying to catch you out— Is that what you mean?"

"Something after that fashion . . . And it's up to

me—and Mr. Sayer who, you might say, is our referee—
to try and turn the tables."

"Ooh, that sounds like fun," said Miss Arnold, wide-
eyed. "I'll make sure I get Mr. Sayer here as fast as I
can."

"I should be most obliged if you would— Now,
here's the description of the person I want you to keep
an eye out for . . ."

Strictly according to plan and immediately following the pertinent ceremonials, Miss Gidding General was brought along to have her fortune told by Madame Herrmann.

There was, thought the clairvoyante as Karen Wheeler came through the curtain, something almost sacrificial about the girl's appearance. Her floor-length white organdie dress had a high Victorian collar, a pintucked bodice and filmy leg-of-mutton sleeves. A white satin sash which bore the legend *Miss Gidding General* lettered in gold was pinned on her right shoulder. On her dark head was a coronet of Cécile Brunner roses.

Photographs were taken. A youthful, disinterested local reporter fired the stock set of questions at the clairvoyante with one eye continually cocked to see if someone more worthy of his attention should suddenly emerge through the curtain. There was a lot of cross-talk between Lady Felton and someone whom she referred to as *'m'dear'*, then as abruptly and unceremoniously as they had appeared, and almost as if some secret signal to depart had been given, the Miss Gidding General entourage started to drift away—first Lady Felton and *m'dear* and then the Press photographer and the reporter with Miss Gidding General between them.

As Karen was about to pass through the curtain, she hesitated momentarily and looked back at the clairvoyante whose attention was elsewhere and con-

centrated wholly on the cards which the girl had laid
out on the table, more under instruction from the
photographer than from the clairvoyante: then, smiling faintly, Karen moved on after the others. Miss
Arnold waited for her to pass, then sprang forward
and parted the curtain.

"Are you ready to continue, Madame?" she enquired.

Mrs. Charles raised her head and gazed absently at
the eager face before her. "No, Miss Arnold," she said
at length. "Not just for the moment. I should like to
have a few more minutes to catch my breath. . . ."

Miss Arnold nodded sympathetically. "I thought
Lady Felton was most inconsiderate. You'd think a
person in her position, a lady of her high standing in
society, would show a little respect and consideration
for someone of your fine sensibilities. I'll close down
the booth for twenty minutes and fetch us both a nice
cup of tea."

"That would be most agreeable, thank you, Miss
Arnold. I wonder, though, if first you'd be kind
enough to find Mr. Sayer and ask him if he could
spare me a moment or two of his time?"

"It would be my pleasure, Madame," Miss Arnold
assured her, and black gown flapping about her legs,
off she went to find him.

"That was quick! I thought it would take a lot longer
than that for you to deliberate and come up with
your findings."

Mrs. Charles looked up at the speaker whose florid
complexion gave some indication of the warmth of
the day.

"There isn't time for that, Superintendent," she

said. "As so often happens in circumstances such as these, the unexpected has happened. I've been caught totally unawares."

David Sayer drew out a chair and sat down at the table. He mopped his streaming brow with his handkerchief. "You, Madame? Never! I refuse to believe it."

"That's very loyal of you, but nevertheless, the fact remains: I've been extremely short-sighted. I should've known, *seen*, what was going to happen. I only hope we're not too late."

"Too late for what?"

"To save the life of the third and final Tarot victim." She looked annoyed. "I knew something was wrong when I chose the combination . . . *The World* followed by *The Sun*—you'll remember that I told you that this would be the Tarot murderer's final combination of cards." She shook her head. "*The World* has to be, is *my* card in this unpleasant little game, Superintendent. In the light of the fresh knowledge that I've gained from my reading of these three cards that you see before me, I now believe that the combination of cards for the Tarot murderer's final victim will be *The Sun*, as I've already predicted, followed by *Death* . . . in this instance, *Death* is the card that will be left on the body of the victim for the police to find. And it's with this special combination, *The Sun* preceding *Death*, that the Tarot murderer will express his radiating universal triumph on that person's death."

He gave her an odd look. "You're not talking about Miss Gidding General, Karen Wheeler? *She's* not next on the list? I thought you said—"

"I know what I said, Superintendent," she interrupted him, "and from that, the suspicions I had about

her, I should've known that there was every possibility
that she'd be victim No. 3. And yet . . ."

She looked down at the cards on the table, all three
of which were inverted number cards from Swords, the
suit in the Minor or Lesser Arcana which correlates
with strife and ill-fortune.

"No," she went on after a moment. "I need more
time to be sure, time to quiet my mind. But in the
meantime, you must act immediately if that girl's life
is to be saved. I think we may be in time. I see nothing
to suggest that she's already received *The Sun* from
her adversary. I deeply regret that the circumstances
precluded the use of my special twenty-four card
spread, which gives a deep, penetrating analysis of the
future. I'd know then exactly what lies ahead of the
girl, and how best to act upon that knowledge. By
comparison, the method I was obliged to use here is
more of a lightning sketch, extremely accurate as far
as it goes, but lacking all the finer details. More guess-
work is required on the part of the clairvoyante to
fill in the gaps. Fortunately, having met the girl on a
previous occasion had experienced her astral vibrations, that task will be somewhat simplified, but it
will still take time . . ."

"Wouldn't it be simpler to fetch her back on some
pretext or other to do this special reading of yours?"

Mrs. Charles was staring at the cards. Then she
tapped one, the two of Swords, with her right forefinger. "*Duplicity*," she murmured. "How stupid of
me not to think of that before. . . ."

She looked up quickly. "I beg your pardon, Superintendent. You said something—?"

"Get the girl back . . . Between the two of us, I'm

sure we can come up with some plausible excuse for your wanting to see her again."

The clairvoyante was shaking her head. "Karen Wheeler won't be tricked into coming back here to see me. She has far too much to hide, more even than I suspected. It was only the Press photographer's insistence that he should take a photograph of Karen with me while I was ostensibly reading the Tarot for her, that I was able to get her to lay out any cards at all for me. She doesn't take me very seriously, but like most sceptics, when faced with a choice would nevertheless prefer to walk round the ladder rather than under it."

She went on with a smile:

"Fortunately, I'd expected something of the kind, and had a second, specially prepared pack of Tarot cards ready and waiting in case of just such a contingency. As you can see, there are only three cards in this reading, the first to be laid down by the seeker, Karen, representing the past, the second the present, and the third the fture; and the secret of this method— my own—of reading these three cards lies in the skill with which the Tarot is prepared before being handed out to the seeker to shuffle. Years of experience have gone into the evolution of the precise sequence in which I place each one of the seventy-eight cards in the Tarot before giving it to the seeker to shuffle, and although, as I've already explained to you, the bolder outlines only of the past, the present and future are revealed, the special preparation of the Tarot guarantees its accuracy."

David looked mystified. "It's all above my head, I'm afraid, Madame. But I'll take your word for it. If you say that Karen Wheeler is the Tarot murderer's next victim, then I won't argue with you."

"Thank you, Superintendent. Now we must apply ourselves to the problem of what to do, how best to go about saving her life." She paused, frowning. "If only people realised how dangerous it is to dabble with this kind of treachery. One simply cannot play games with murderers." She sighed. "Karen will be safe enough today, here in the limelight. But what of tomorrow and the next day and the day thereafter?"

They lapsed into a long, thoughtful silence. At length, David said:

"We've really only got the one course of action open to us. You'll appreciate that I can't go to the police with our suspicions. Admittedly, they called in Roxeth to give his views on the meanings of the Tarot cards, but that was normal police procedure. One mustn't infer that that points to a change of heart by the police who are, Madame, with all due respect, by nature and out of necessity born sceptics when it comes to dealing with people like yourself. So that leaves us with the victim, Karen Wheeler. I think—if you'll forgive the pun—that we've got to lay our cards on the table . . . Face her with what you suspect about her and then try to put the fear of the very devil himself into her by telling her straight that she's next."

Mrs. Charles nodded slowly. "I'm not happy about it: she's not the kind to scare easily which means it could so easily backfire on us. However, like you, I can see no other way around the problem: it's a risk we've got to take. But if we fail to alert her to the danger which faces her and she goes to the Tarot murderer and warns him about us, then I suspect that that could see the end of our hopes to see him brought to justice for his crimes. My trump card has always been knowing who he is. Play that card now—and I agree, play it we must to try and save that girl's life—and I'm not at all sure that this won't mean that the Tarot murderer wins the game."

"You *know* who the Tarot murderer is?"

She sighed. "*Suspect* I know, Superintendent. It was perhaps a little premature of me to say otherwise, even if he did as good as tell me himself who he was."

There was a short pause.

"Well?" he said. "You're not going to confide in me?"

She hesitated. "I'm not yet completely satisfied that the evidence of my ears is correct."

"I'll be most surprised if you're mistaken, Madame," he said thinly.

"That's all very flattering, Superintendent, and I'm deeply touched by your faith in my abilities. However, after having given the matter some considerable thought, and for deeply personal reasons, I've decided never to reveal to anyone the identity of the Tarot murderer. That the Tarot murderer must do himself. I've told you as much as I ever propose to tell anyone of my knowledge of these murders and of the man who has committed them. In the past you've found it in yourself to trust my judgment of these matters, and once again I beg your indulgence."

He dwelt for a moment on what she had said, only the latter part of which he was prepared to accept without argument; but as he prepared his case, a strange uneasiness came over him, and after a minute or two's further thought—and for reasons he was at a loss to explain to himself—he finally decided to let it rest. "Very well, Madame," he said quietly. He paused and smiled crookedly. "I am your ever-willing and devoted servant. Tell me what you think I ought to do."

"Find the girl and see if you can get her to come back here with you."

"And if she's doesn't want to know?"

"Then we'll have to go to her . . . after the fete is over. As I've said, she's safe enough here today."

"Tea up!" a chirpy voice, Miss Arnold's, called from the other side of the curtain.

"I'll see you later with Karen," whispered David.

That was never to be.

After leaving Mrs. Charles, David intermingled with the throngs of people milling about the gardens adjoining the hospital and began to search for Miss Gidding General. On his second time round, almost half-an-hour later, he met up with his wife, Jean, and asked her if she had seen the girl anywhere.

"She was over there," Jean replied, pointing to a small marquee some distance away. "They're judging the home produce. It was so crowded and hot in there that I got out of it." She fanned her face with some advertising literature which she had had pressed upon her during the course of the morning. She was a pretty, feminine woman, a year or two younger than her friend, Mary Sutherland. She went on: "Right now, I'm looking for a small patch of lawn under a nice shady tree and a long cool drink."

"The trees are over there, behind you," said David, grinning, "but you might have to forget about the cool drink. I heard someone say they've run out of ice."

Jean grimaced. Then, curiously, she asked, "What do you want with the lovely Miss Gidding General?"

"I thought that on behalf of all the menfolk in Gidding, I should tell her how beautiful we all think she is," he replied, straight-faced.

"I shouldn't bother if I were you: I think she already knows— Hang on!" she exclaimed. "Don't rush off. I'll come with you."

"No," he said quickly. "I'd rather you didn't."

"I'm quite sure you'd rather—" she broke off, the smile on her lips fading. David had been jumpy all morning . . . just like he was the time he and Mrs. Charles—Jean's eyes widened with surprise. *Those two villains were cooking something up again!* "It's as well," she sighed, a mischievous twinkle in her eyes, "that I'm not a jealous woman, isn't it? And I'm not talking about little Miss Gorgeous-and-don't-I-know-it, either. Well," she said peremptorily, "don't keep our illustrious clairvoyante waiting!"

He shot her a quick, anxious glance.

"You can take that look off your face," she said airily. "My lips are sealed . . . May my lemon meringue pie not even rate a special mention if I ever breathe a word to a living soul! I haven't seen you . . . at least," she added with a grin, "not since the last time."

He grinned back. "Remind me to buy you a nice, long cool drink some time."

"I'll do that," she called to his retreating back.

Miss Gidding General was nowhere to be seen anywhere near the home produce tables. David turned to leave the crowded marquee and bumped straight into James and Mary Sutherland.

"You look," observed Mary, "as if you've lost a fiver and found—"

David interrupted her sharply. "I was told that Miss Gidding General was in here."

"Well worth a second look, too, old son," chuckled James Sutherland, a big man whose shaggy eyebrows badly needed a trim. "A right little cracker!"

"I think she's gone home," said Mary.

"*Gone home?* How can she go home?" exclaimed David irritably. "I mean, what for? I thought she'd be here all day!"

"For goodness' sake," said Mary laughingly. "You don't have to get so excited about it. She could be back. It's probably only nervous tension . . . too much excitement."

"She's been taken ill?" asked David quickly.

Mary gave him a surprised look. David was snapping at her as if she were a suspect in a murder case. "If you're going to be like that about it, David," she said thoughtfully.

"Forgive me, Mary," he apologised curtly. "You're talking to a very old, frustrated man—"

"Old at fifty-two?" she exclaimed.

David curbed his growing impatience and forced himself to smile. "Older than I was when I was twenty-one," he said.

"Why, David," she said playfully. "I almost believe that you're actually in danger of becoming a dirty old man!"

James Sutherland, who was standing a little to one side listening to the exchange, studied his friend closely. Something wrong here, he thought. If David didn't simmer down, he'd have another heart attack.

"Everyone's got a different story about why the girl took off so suddenly," James spoke out abruptly. "Those young people over there," he went on, pointing them out. "The fair-haired girl . . . Didn't I hear you say, dear," he addressed his wife, "that she's one of Miss Gidding General's friends?"

"So Lady Felton told me when she said that Miss Gidding General had been taken ill. I wouldn't really know myself."

"Attractive girl," observed James, eyeing the blonde.

"What's got into you men today?" exclaimed Mary. She grabbed her husband by the arm and marched him into the marquee. "You come along with me, my boy, and cast your admiring glances at the voluptuous sensuality of the prize-winning vegetable marrows. . . ."

David went over to the young people and spoke to Rosemary McAfee-Smith, the fair-haired girl who had been pointed out to him by his friend.

"I understand that you're friendly with Karen Wheeler," he began.

"Yes, that's right: we share a flat together," she said wonderingly. (Did she know this man?) "Why?"

"I wonder if I might have a few words with you in private? I won't keep you a moment."

She widened her eyes a little, then shrugged and said, "Sure, why not." She flashed a grin at her friends. "Don't run away any of you. I shan't be long."

David and the girl picked their way slowly around the heat prostrated bodies sprawling on the lawn to the shade of an old chestnut tree.

"My name," he explained, "is David Sayer. I'm an ex-police superintendent, retired through ill-health, and a friend of Mrs. Charles . . . Madame Adele Herrmann."

A suspicious light showed in the girl's eyes but she made no comment and waited for him to continue.

"Why did Karen leave the fete? Is she really sick or was that simply an excuse?"

The girl drew back from him. There was a fixed expression on her face and her voice took on a warning note. "Look, Mr. ex-policeman Thayer, Sayer, whatever . . . I don't have to answer any of your questions. I mightn't know a lot about the rights of the ordinary average citizen, but that much I do know. If you've got any questions to ask me about Karen, you ask

Karen to answer them, not me. She's quite capable of speaking for herself."

"And if I'm too late?" he asked evenly. "If the Tarot murderer has already made her his third victim—?"

She gave a start. Fear showed in her eyes. "What are you talking about?" she demanded.

"She's at home, is she? At the flat . . . on her own?" He started to walk away.

"Just a minute!" She ran after him. "What was that you said about the Tarot murderer?"

"Hey, Rosie!" one of her friends called to her. "Where are you going?"

"I'll see you later," she called back, and quickly caught up with David who pushed on resolutely through the crowds, ignoring her.

"She—Karen—got a special delivery," panted Rosie. "I was with her when the boy rode up and said he had a special delivery letter for her. I thought it was someone sending her congratulations—you know, for winning the Miss Gidding General contest. Anyway," the girl went on breathlessly, "she opened it . . . well, *half* opened it—sort of ripped up the flap on the envelope; then she . . . well, she suddenly went very pale and pushed past everyone and said she felt sick."

They were out in the street, David now a good two yards ahead of Rosie who was having to run to keep even that close to him.

Ignoring the stares they were getting, the girl continued:

"She rushed off to the toilets and I went after her to make sure that she was all right." Rosie paused to catch her breath, pressing her fingers into her left side where she had begun to get a sharp pain. Then

she raced on after David. When she was close enough
for him to hear what she said, she went on:

"By the time I got to the toilets, Karen was already
locked inside one of the cubicles. I sang out to her
that it was me, and was she okay, and she called back
that everything was fine. Then I heard her tearing
something up . . . She flushed the toilet several times;
and then she came out."

David disappeared round a corner and it was a moment or two before Rosie was able to continue.

"Karen said she had a bit of a headache—she gets
dreadful migraines—and that she thought she should
slip home and take something for it before it got any
worse. I offered to go for her, but she was deafer than
you are . . . she just went charging off home, didn't
hear a word I said," she complained. "So I thought,
'Well, be like that if you want to: see if I care!', and
I went back and sort of made apologies to Lady Felton
for her . . . said she'd probably be back later. I didn't
think so myself. Karen only gets her headaches when
she's hopping mad about something. . . ."

David unlatched the gate to the garden-flat at No. 12
Roedene Close and waited for Rosie to catch up. Then
he said, "So what you're saying now is that Karen
wasn't sick at all, she was angry about something—the
special delivery she'd received?"

"Look," said Rose breathlessly, leaning bodily
against the gate and rubbing her left side. "I know
Karen pretty well . . . we share a flat, right? When the
colour drains out of her face and then the next thing
she's talking about is one of her heads, she's got her
knickers in a twist about something."

"You don't think she could've been upset . . . afraid,
perhaps?"

"No, I don't. Karen doesn't frighten easily. She just gets mad!"

"You've got no idea what was in the envelope that was delivered to her?"

The girl shrugged. "I could make a shrewd guess. Some of us thought that as a mark of respect to her dead friend, Miriam—her *best* friend—who really won the Miss Gidding General contest, Karen should've stepped down and not accepted the title. One or two of the other girls were quite hostile towards her when she made her decision to go ahead and accept it, especially as it had always been fairly obvious to everyone that she hadn't been too pleased that she'd only got second place to Miriam. I thought that one of them had sent her some kind of sarcastic note congratulating her on her win. But—" She paused. Then, haltingly: "What did you mean about Karen being the Tarot murderer's third victim?"

"Do you have a key?" he enquired, ignoring the question.

She nodded and got it out of the orange canvas hold-all she had slung across one shoulder.

"Make sure that Karen is all right," he said tersely, "and then I'd be obliged if you'd tell her that I should like to have a word with her."

The girl shrugged, unlocked the door and then disappeared into a room off the hall calling her flatmate's name.

A brief silence was followed by an inarticulate sound, neither a scream nor a call for help, then a moment later, Rosie staggered blindly into the hall moaning something which sounded like, '*Oh, my God!*'

David brushed past her and went through the sitting-room to the girls' bedroom.

The room was reasonably neat and orderly, the beds made. Karen was lying outstretched on the one farthest from the door. The coronet of Cécile Brunner roses had been removed from her head and placed on her hands which were crossed over her breast. On top of the coronet was a Tarot card, card number thirteen in the Major Arcana . . . *Death*.

David stood by the bed looking down at the girl. But for the ugly little hole in her right temple, she could have been sleeping peacefully.

XXI   THE WORLD
The Attainment of the Ultimate Goal

Mrs. Charles listened gravely to what David Sayer had to tell her. When he had finished speaking, the man whom he had introduced as Chief Superintendent Merton, cleared his throat and said, "I think, Madame, that the time has come for some explanations."

The clairvoyante glanced at David who, having correctly read the question in her eyes, indicated by a small, barely discernible movement of his head that he had adhered strictly to the facts and that he had not told the police that she had professed to know the identity of the Tarot murderer.

"Explanations, Superintendent Merton?" she said smoothly. "By all means. What it is that you wish to know?"

"I should like you to tell me, Madame," said the slightly-balding, steely-eyed Chief Superintendent, "how it is that you were able, with such precise accuracy, to predict the murder of Miss Karen Wheeler, even down to a correct description of the card which the so-called Tarot murderer would leave on her body."

"You require me to interpret the Tarot for you— the three cards in the murdered girl's reading?"

"That will not be necessary, thank you, Madame," said Merton abruptly. "Mr. Sayer has already outlined the general content of your prediction from the Tarot cards which you say the murdered girl dealt from the pack while you and she were being photographed together this morning. The recognised authority on the

Tarot who's been assisting us with our enquiries into
these murders will be called in again to give his expert
opinion of the meanings of those particular cards,"
he informed her, a trifle insolently.

"Rupert Roxeth?" enquired the clairvoyante bland-
ly.

"That is correct," he replied.

"You'll forgive my impertinence, Chief Superintendent, but calling in Rupert Roxeth hasn't proved
in the past to be the way in which to apprehend the
Tarot murderer any more than it will in the future."

"Indeed," said Merton coldly.

"Don't let your prejudice against that which defies
your understanding blind you to the possibility that
someone like myself—a member of what you undoubtedly would describe as 'the lunatic fringe'—might just
happen to know what she's talking about," said the
clairvoyante with unusual severity.

"I apologise if I've offended you, Madame," said
Merton archly. "It wasn't my intention to be rude.
Although a relative newcomer to the district, I'm fully
aware of your reputation as a clairvoyante and that
you're held in very high esteem by many of my col-
leagues at police headquarters. However, this latest
murder leaves me in no doubt that we are dealing with
a homicidal maniac—a man who has killed three times
and will go on killing until he's stopped. That,
Madame, is my difficulty . . . To prevent more Tarot
murders and to allay the fears of every young woman
living and working within a twenty-five mile radius
of Gidding when the country at large gets to hear of
the latest in this series of murders."

"There will be no more Tarot murders, Chief Superintendent," said Mrs. Charles quietly.

"I am relieved to hear it, Madame," he said thinly. "But you'll appreciate that I cannot take that risk and must therefore use every source of information available to me in the furtherance of that aim, including Rupert Roxeth."

"Have you acquainted Professor Roxeth with the news of this latest Tarot murder?" she enquired.

"No, Madame. For the moment, you, Mr. Sayer, the dead girl's flat-mate—Miss McAfee-Smith—myself (and my men, of course), are the only ones who know anything about it. At Mr. Sayer's request, I came straight here to see you—"

"And the Tarot murderer," she interrupted the Chief Superintendent abstractedly. "You mustn't forget him. He knows . . . And if we are patient, very patient, he'll come here today to see me. To gloat."

Merton flicked his eyes over David before saying, "Gloat? I don't think I understand . . ."

"This is a game—a game between the Tarot murderer and me . . . one which came into being long before the body of the first Tarot victim was discovered. A battle of wits, the Tarot murderer's against mine . . . that's what the Tarot murders have really been all about—a playing off of one person against another."

Merton looked at David who said, "I think Madame Herrmann is right, Clive. It makes sense to me."

"But that is not to imply that the Tarot murderer's victims were picked at random," the clairvoyante went on. "Victim No. 1, Miriam Noad, I believe rejected him; Victim No. 2, Lorna Lock, made a nuisance of herself; and Victim No. 3, Karen Wheeler, discovered his identity and tried—or was trying, I think you'll ultimately discover—to blackmail him."

"You have some very definite idea then, Madame,"

observed Merton shrewdly, "who the Tarot murderer is."

"He was so sure of himself that he deliberately over-played his hand and revealed his identity to me, told me to my face that he was the Tarot murderer."

Merton frowned. "Am I to take it that he has no idea that you know who he is?"

"I think we can safely assume that he's as confident as ever," she replied. "He wouldn't have dared to risk committing the final Tarot murder right under every-one's nose if he'd felt anything other than completely secure in his belief that he has nothing to fear from me. Or from the police," she added, eyebrows raised meaningfully.

The curtain rustled and with a nervous little cough, Miss Arnold excused herself: then addressing herself to Mrs. Charles, and in an awed voice, she said that there were quite a number of people queuing to see her and asked should she tell everyone that the booth was closed for the day. Miss Arnold's eyes were very big and round which seemed to indicate that she had overheard sufficient of the foregoing conversation for her to have come to the startling but erroneous con-clusion that Madame Herrmann was involved in some kind of criminal conspiracy and likely at any moment now to be led away under close arrest.

Miss Arnold's voice dropped to a whisper. "I don't know if it matters now, Madame, but that person you asked me to watch out for . . . well, he's out there." She twitched her eyes over her shoulder without mov-ing her head. "Third in the queue," she whispered hoarsely, as if the drama of the moment were proving too much for her vocal chords and they were failing under the strain of it all. "He's been waiting for some time."

Mrs. Charles raised her eyebrows interrogatively. "Well, Chief Superintendent . . . Do we play out the Tarot murderer's game to its natural conclusion?"

Merton looked at David who returned his gaze stoically and said nothing. At length, the Chief Superintendent came back to Mrs. Charles and said, "It occurs to me, Madame, that I have very little to lose. What would you suggest that we should do?"

"Leave now, immediately—as naturally as you can and without showing any undue interest, if possible, in those who are waiting to see me. Find yourselves somewhere quiet to sit; and then why not have a nice cup of tea while you wait? There are two people in the queue ahead of our quarry and they'll be with me for approximately ten to fifteen minutes each. After, say, twenty minutes, you should start to keep a discreet watch on the booth to make sure that our man is still in the queue and the next to come in here."

"We'll move up as soon as we see him go through the curtain," said Merton, nodding.

Mrs. Charles looked at Miss Arnold whose eyes were now like saucers. "Once you've shown him in, Miss Arnold, I should like you to close down the booth for a while . . . Perhaps you could call out to me that you're going for some tea."

The clairvoyante switched her gaze back on to Merton. "It's imperative that he should think that he and I are alone together: he won't admit to anything while he thinks there's a chance that Miss Arnold may overhear his conversation with me."

Merton turned to Miss Arnold. "Do you think

you're up to this, Miss Arnold? You must realise, from
what has been said here, how important it is that this
man isn't forewarned in any way."

Mrs. Charles said, "I'm quite sure that we can rely
on Miss Arnold to assist me now as ably as she has
throughout the earlier part of the day."

Miss Arnold was flushed with pleasure.

"You can depend on me, Madame . . . gentlemen,"
she assured them solemnly.

The men moved towards the curtain.

"Over to you, Madame," said Merton.

She was looking not at the Chief Superintendent
but beyond him to David. The expression in her eyes
puzzled both men. She looked so very sad, thought
David.

The two men walked casually in the direction of the
refreshments marquee where afternoon-tea was now
being served.

"Well," said Merton when they were well clear of
the fortune-telling booth. "Who would be your choice
for Tarot murderer out of that happy, chatty little
group standing a bit beyond what appeared to me to
be customers one and two? Amery Walters? His son,
Peter? John Carrington-Jones—finder of Tarot victim
No. 2? That vet. chap, Sutherland, perhaps? And what
about that leading pillar of society, our foxy friend,
Rupert Roxeth, Esquire?"

"Anyone's guess," said David absently. Privately he
could do a whole lot better than that. The parting
look in Mrs. Charles' eyes haunted him. She wouldn't
be sad about Roxeth, so he was in the clear. Amery
Walters? Why be sad about him? Peter Walters and
young John? Perhaps . . . because of their youth and

the lives which still lay ahead of them. James Sutherland? Well, that was too ridiculous for words! David smiled faintly. 'Mother Hen' Mary, maybe, but not— He paused mid-thought and suddenly he had his answer, knew why Mrs. Charles hadn't wished to disclose to him the identity of the Tarot murderer. . . .

XXII THE FOOL
The Consummate Folly

"Hullo, John," said Mrs. Charles. "Please come in and sit down."

John Carrington-Jones grinned at her. "Who are we today? Mrs. Charles or Madame Adele?"

He drew out a chair and sat down.

"How is your little problem with Peter coming along?" she enquired, smiling. "Is the applied psychology working?"

"Up to a point. We've swapped turns," he said, folding his arms on the table and leaning on them. "I wanted to have a word with you first."

"Not another bribe?"

His eyebrows rose. "Aunt Mary crossed your palm with silver?"

"Something of the sort."

"And you let her bribe you?"

Mrs. Charles responded with a fleeting smile.

He studied her thoughtfully for a moment and then he, too, smiled fleetingly. "No, you wouldn't, would you? You know, you're the nearest I'd say that I . . . any of us—the people who've had their fortunes told by you today—are ever likely to come to the real genuine thing."

The blue eyes were mildly amused. "But even I fall short?"

"I don't mean to be offensive, but it's all a bit of a con. trick, isn't it? Looking at pretty picture cards and gazing in crystal balls. Just between you and me, that applied psychology you mentioned a moment ago . . .

that's really what it's all about, isn't it? The cards and the crystal—they're just the frosting on the cake."

The clairvoyante gave him a long, contemplative look. Then she smiled. "I presume," she said, "that Miss Arnold accepted fifty pence from you for a reading of the Tarot?"

At the sound of her name, Miss Arnold popped her head through the curtain. "Just going for a cup of tea," she announced nervously, her eyes fixed on Mrs. Charles and flustered colour rising on her face. "I'm closing down the booth for twenty minutes."

As if on an elastic band, Miss Arnold's head snapped back and disappeared. A chair was knocked over in her haste to quit the booth.

"Now, John," said Mrs. Charles quietly. "Your reading. . . ."

"You're not going to defend yourself over what I've said?" he asked, eyeing her mockingly.

"No," she replied. "I care only about what I think of myself and my ability to exercise the extraordinary powers with which I've been blest. Your good opinion of me—or that of anyone else for me—is of no consequence to me. I am, and have always held myself to be, answerable to no one but myself."

"I really believe you mean that," he said. "And that's where you score over Roxeth. If I'd said the things to him that I've just said to you, he'd be flapping about like a demented parrot, feathers flying everywhere."

She pushed the pack of Tarot cards towards him. "Cut the cards, John," she said quietly. "Just the once."

"Now what?" he asked, following out her instruction.

"Turn up the next card and lay it face up on the table."

As he turned the card over, the smile on his face became fixed, rigid with shock.

"*Vingt-deux,*" she said softly. "*The Fool,* inverted."

He stared at her for almost a full minute without saying anything, then threw back his head and laughed. Finally, his laughter spent, he said, "Inverted?"

"The foolish, reckless Tarot murderer has reached the end of the road. The game is over."

The mocking look was back in his eyes. "You really are a lot cleverer than Roxeth. I treated you both fairly, gave you exactly the same clues. I know my French pronunciation is pretty lousy, but you spotted that the name I gave my dog, Vanda, was really meant to be *Vingt-deux,* the French for twenty-two, and connected it with *The Fool,* the twenty-second picture card in the Tarot. Roxeth never twigged . . . saw the connection between the two. I call my dog a fool, but he's an even bigger one," he said disgustedly. "Gets right up my nose."

"That's why you tried to set the two of us off against one another, isn't it? That and your hatred of him over his indifferent attitude towards cruelty to animals . . . the brutal manner in which he would have Mr. Walters train his horses if Mr. Walters were agreeable."

He smiled crookedly. "Your name is poison to Roxeth. He talks about you constantly, you know . . . Nothing that you'd be flattered to hear repeated, of course. I got fed up listening to him go on about himself . . . what a smart fellow he is and how little you know. Aunt Mary gave me the idea for getting him to

put a sock in it about you and the Tarot once and for
all. She kept on and on about how clever you were
and I thought. 'Right . . . let's put it to the test, shall
we?'."

"This was last Christmas— After Miriam Noad decided to put her career ahead of you?"

His face darkened with suppressed rage. "Yes.
Miriam, herself, was somewhat blunter . . . I think
she was a lot like you and could see what only one
other person has ever been able to see about me. I'm
not a nice person, you know. I'm very fond of animals
—horses and dogs—but I've never been able to work
up much enthusiasm over people. Not even for Miriam. Once I'd made up my mind about Roxeth and
you, and had decided that she'd be my first victim, I
enjoyed every moment of it . . . the months of plan-
ning, the actual physical act of killing someone, reading all the things people said about me (the murderer)
afterwards, going to the special service that milk-sop
Povey held for her at St. Luke's . . . sitting there right
at the back of the church where no one would see me
. . . watching them, those spineless drop-outs who lean
on The Good Samaritan and people like Miriam who
then misguidedly see their kind as their mission in
life." He shook his head slowly. "I couldn't understand it—how Miriam could prefer the company of
people like that—to *mine*.

"None of it would've happened if Peter had been
able to come home for Christmas. He got glandular
fever and spent Christmas in hospital in London.
When I look back now, I don't know how I stood it . . .
Roxeth strutting about like a stuffed peacock and
spouting all his precious nonsense about himself. Aunt
Mary chattering incessantly about you (no doubt be-

cause she knew that I'd become friendly with Roxeth through Peter and his family, and thought that she was being very with it by talking about a subject which—heaven knows why!—she imagined I was suddenly taking an avid interest in) : then all that time wasted listening to Miriam go on about The Good Samaritan and all the good works that get done there . . . in the hope, of course, that I'd be so inspired that I couldn't wait to lend a hand. Unfortunately, I've never cared about anyone but myself, and everything that I do is always calculated on the greatest possible benefit to No. 1," he admitted arrogantly. "And then to cap it all, that wretched little pest Lorna turned up in Gidding and made a nuisance of herself."

"It was you she liked—cared about—wasn't it? She kept going out to Mr. Walters' stables last Christmas looking for you, not Peter."

He shrugged. "Miriam was about the only female who didn't throw herself at me. It's probably what attracted me to her. The challenge. When Lorna sabotaged Peter's play, she was really getting at me. I coproduced it with him."

"I suspected as much," said the clairvoyante. "The initial necklet she used to wear . . . It was Miriam's, wasn't it? One you gave her last Christmas."

He shrugged again, then thrust his hands into the pockets of his jeans and leaned back in his chair.

"Lorna knew I'd given it to Miriam. She followed me one day to a jeweller's shop in Gidding . . . watched me buy it—knew it was for Miriam—and was so jealous that she fought Miriam for it down at The Good Samaritan. Lorna had got into the habit of following either Miriam or me—or the two of us—about, but it was just by chance that she went along to The Good

Samaritan one Sunday morning last December looking for a meal and found Miriam there wearing the necklet. And Miriam cared so much about it—the gift *I'd* given her—that she let Lorna get away with stealing it from her. Lorna never went back there again after that in case there was trouble over the necklet."

"You tore it from her throat after you'd drowned her?"

"I took back what was mine. Miriam obviously never wanted it, and it was never meant for Lorna."

"Tell me about the night you killed Miriam."

He grinned crookedly. "You're the one with the crystal ball. You tell me."

"As you wish," said the clairvoyante quietly. "At the end of term, you came here to your god-parents, as has been your custom since your father was posted abroad, and you made your first move in the game that you'd decided some seven or eight months ago to play with Rupert Roxeth and me. You sent Miriam Noad a card from the Tarot—*The Tower of Destruction*—which I broadly interpreted to indicate the death of everything that you'd ever felt for her."

His eyes widened. "Go on," he invited. "I'm listening."

"Miriam didn't understand what the card meant—and had no idea who had sent it to her—so she took it along to The Good Samaritan and showed it to someone there, a down-and-out known as Scottie the sculptor—"

"Incredible, wasn't it?" he said, shaking his head wonderingly. "That man's brain was so addled with drink that he couldn't correctly connect two halves of a simple sentence and yet Miriam took it to him."

"What did you expect her to do with it?"

"I thought she'd show it to Karen, her flat-mate. Karen—a dedicated social climber," he interpolated with a sneer, "used to go out to Roxeth's parties. I met Miriam through her—not at one of the parties. As far as I know, Miriam never went out to Roxeth's place with the other social workers from The Good Samaritan . . . Roxeth is another one for good works: he'd never get his hands soiled in the way that the Miriams of this world would, but he's got a finger in the pie of most of the charitable organisations in and around Gidding. Miriam's nursing and her studies didn't seem to leave her much time for socialising . . . As a matter of fact, The Good Samaritan was her social life. That was where she spent most of her free time, and it was also where I first met her. I called in one Saturday afternoon to see Karen about Roxeth's Christmas party—I was taking her to it—and Miriam was there. Karen introduced us and our friendship 'blossomed', as the romanticists would say, from there."

"Karen was familiar with the Tarot?"

"No, but she knew Roxeth was, and I expected her to take the card out to him."

For some minutes, Mrs. Charles had been aware that she and John were no longer alone and that there was someone—a person or persons—standing beyond the curtain listening in to their conversation; but John's guard was now completely down. Insensitive to the danger about him, he went on:

"I found out later that things weren't quite the same between Karen and Miriam: they weren't so chummy with one another any more and hadn't been since Christmas when Miriam gave me the shove. They had some kind of argument over me . . . Karen, of course, was jealous of Miriam: she would've given anything to have been in her shoes."

Mrs. Charles nodded slowly. That, she suspected, would be the disagreement that Rosie had mentioned, the one which she had walked in on during the night out by some of the hospital staff. Rosie had been right the first time. Miriam and Karen's squabble had, as Rosie had thought, been about a man.

"What did Scottie tell Miriam about the Tarot card?"

"He didn't know what it meant. But he said he'd try to find out. So Miriam left the card with him and then he promptly forgot about it."

"Not quite," said Mrs. Charles. "He made a wood carving of the card."

The young man eyed her coldly. "As I was about to say, he couldn't remember why he had the card, so he did the thing that came most naturally to him and made a wood carving of it."

"Possibly . . . But I also think he guessed that it was a bad card and that you had sent it to Miriam."

"He had his lucid moments," he conceded off-handedly. "Or so they tell me."

"What led him to suspect you? The fight he witnessed between Lorna and Miriam over the necklet?"

He gave her a thoughtful look. Then he shrugged a little and said, "Scottie heard Lorna scream at Miriam that she'd live to regret the day that she took up with me." He laughed hollowly. "Miriam didn't *live* to regret it. She *died* for it. The hospital made it easy for me. They packed her off home for a rest. I was pleased about that," he went on reflectively, a disturbingly vacant look in his eye. "I liked the idea of

the Tarot murderer (that wasn't how I pictured myself then, but I'm becoming used to thinking of myself
in those terms) : however, as I was saying, it pleased
me to think of the Tarot murderer striking at random
. . . I could imagine the terror spreading out from
Gidding like the rays of the sun. I knew that Miriam,
without The Good Samaritan to turn to for something
to do, would probably go to a disco on the Saturday
night, so after I'd finished work at the stables that day,
I said I wasn't feeling too well and that I was going
straight home to bed. Some of the other lads were
going into Gidding—"

"Peter Walters knew nothing of your friendship
with Miriam?"

"Lorna was the only one at the stables who knew
anything about it. My friendship with Miriam was a
very discreet, low-key affair: Miriam was quite para-
noid about getting involved, or being seen to be becoming involved with anyone," he said dryly. "But
to get back to that Saturday night. . . Instead of going
home, I drove over to Hetley Vale, parked a little way
down the street from Miriam's place, and after a while,
she came out. I followed her in the car for a bit (she
was on foot) , and then I caught her up and said I
wanted to speak to her for a few minutes. She said she
didn't want to talk to me, but eventually she got into
the car and told me that she'd give me five minutes
and no more." There was a cruel smile on his lips. "I
did my best not to keep her hanging around for too
long. I told her that I was going to kill her, and do
you know what she said? *'You must be mad!'* "

He gave the clairvoyante a strange look. "She was
right, of course. I am mad. My mother told me so

when I was a small child. She only just arrived in the
nick of time to stop me killing one of my playmates
who'd been torturing a cat." He smiled pitilessly. "I
gave him the same medicine, strung him up by a wire,
too. My mother came along and cut him down. That
was really why Aunt Mary sent David Sayer to see
you about me, you know. Aunt Mary knew about the
incident with the cat—Mother told her—and she was
afraid that something similar had happened at the
stables over one of the animals there, and that Lorna
was somehow involved and I'd killed her for what
she'd done like I'd almost killed that young friend
of mine."

Mrs. Charles regarded him thoughtfully. It came as
no surprise to her that there was more to his god-
mother's concern over him than a fear that he would
not return to university, but she had not suspected
anything quite so horrible as this.

"You left *The Star,* which was inverted," she said
quietly, "with Miriam's body to indicate her shattered
destiny, its combination with *The Tower of Destruction* signifying the abrogation of your feeling for her."

Abruptly, John's mood changed. For some moments,
he stared at the clairvoyante sullenly, without saying
anything. Then he said, very deliberately, "Before I
killed her, I told her that it was I who had sent her
The Tower of Destruction, and then I asked her what
she'd done with it. She told me, so then I knew that
I had to go after Scottie. She knew it, too, and she
laughed at me and said I'd never find him . . . that he
wasn't at The Good Samaritan any more, he'd gone
back to Scotland." His face appeared to thin and the
expression in his eyes became dark and cruel. "I found
him . . . And it was very fitting, I thought, that they

should both finish up the same way—him and his precious Miriam—lying dead in a ditch."

His brow wrinkled and he was quiet for a moment, thinking back. Then he went on:

"I found *The Tower of Destruction* in one of his pockets and I decided to leave it where it was to test Roxeth . . . to see if he would tie it in with the card that I'd left with Miriam. I'd anticipated that Scottie would've been found a lot sooner than he was, and that the police would naturally link him up with her because of their connection with The Good Samaritan," he explained with a careless shrug.

"Why did you bring Lorna to see me?"

What remained of his earlier sullenness dissolved into a sly grin. "Beautiful, wasn't it?" He laughed quietly. "I knew for sure that Lorna would go straight to Roxeth with the Tarot card that I'd left in the pocket of her jacket one day. He, of course, couldn't have been wider of the mark. Then I thought, 'Perfect . . . this time let's see what the opposition has got to say for herself'. But you didn't really commit yourself other than to tell Lorna that *Justice* on its own didn't predict her death. Roxeth had got her so confused with what he'd told her that she didn't know whether she was coming or going, although she was always more than halfway convinced that she was going to die. I hadn't meant to kill her so soon," he confessed, frowning. "She was really uptight about that card, *Justice*. It was pure pleasure watching her suffer. I knew Roxeth was bound to come up with some silly nonsense or other about it, but I never dreamt that he'd be so obliging. Lorna never caught on, you know—realised what it was all about . . . justice, at long last, for all her unpleasantness to everyone and for having stolen Miriam's necklet. Lorna thought it was because of her mother . . . punishment for having caused her death."

"I know," said the clairvoyante. "The poor child must have really suffered."

He gave a short laugh. "Not half as much as she deserved to. An animal has more self-pride than she had." He grimaced. "She was a dirty girl. How she imagined that I'd ever look twice at someone like her . . . She made my flesh crawl! Lived rough—in one of the parks while she was up here, sponged off places like The Good Samaritan (though, as I've already said, she had to give them a very wide berth after she'd swiped the necklet from Miriam and duffed her up), cadged lifts everywhere . . .

"That was what she was doing the night I killed her . . . wandering down the middle of the lane outside Walters' placee, thumbing a lift. I was on my way home alone from the disco in Gidding. Peter had had to stay at home because he'd hurt his ankle in that little fracas we'd had with her in the yard that day after I'd told her what a slattern she was; and the lad who went with me into Gidding, had met up with a girl he knew and gone on somewhere else with her."

He paused and frowned. "I stopped the car and Lorna came over to me and asked if I'd take her into Gidding. She was crying."

There was an odd look on his face, as if he hadn't understood that kind of emotional display from her and still couldn't understand it.

"That blazing row she had with Walters after Old Jack had caught her snooping around the horse-boxes . . ." he went on. "She told me that she'd called Walters a womaniser and a cheat, and dear Miss

Braithwaite something not very nice at all (everybody, including Mrs. Walters, knows what's been going on between Walters and his secretary, but no one ever talked about it). Lorna knew that Walters had meant it when he'd said that she was finished at the stables ... And then she started on to me about *Justice* (the card she'd found in her jacket) and what Roxeth had told her it meant."

There was another very odd expression on his face. "She expected me to *comfort* her . . . that dirty little slut!" He held out his hands and stared at them. "I scrubbed my hands raw after I'd killed her," he said with a shudder. "She repulsed me."

"But first, before you killed her," the clairvoyante reminded him, "you suggested that Rupert Roxeth's interpretation of the card might be wrong, and that she should get a second opinion . . ."

He looked up from his hands and a slow smile spread across his face. "I reminded her that Roxeth was always talking about you, his arch-enemy—Madame Adele Herrmann—and I told her that I secretly suspected that he was frightened of you because you were a hundred times better at the Tarot than he was and he knew it. Lorna swallowed the bait whole."

His head turned a little to one side and he studied the clairvoyante curiously. "What! no exclamation of horror at what a fiend I am?"

Her lack of response brought a quick flash of irritation to his eyes.

"Come up against the lot of us, haven't you? The brain freaks! Aren't you scared . . . *just a little bit*? I've murdered four people, you know; and it's not true what they say, that the first is the hardest—"

"Go on about Lorna," said the clairvoyante evenly.

"What happened after the two of you drove away from my bungalow that night?"

He frowned at her irritably and his mouth set in a thin, straight line. There was a brief, petulant silence; then, at length, he shrugged and said, "I suggested that we should go for a drive down to the beach . . . to where we rode out with the horses every morning." He started to laugh. "She thought I was going to make love to her!"

Again he looked at his hands, inspected his finger-nails. "She bit her nails, you know . . . Like some dirty, scruffy little school-kid. *And she thought I was going to make love to her!*"

He was momentarily silent, thinking it over. Then he went on:

"When we reached the beach, she got out of the car and ran across the sand to the water's edge and started splashing about, kicking up the water at me. Then she stopped larking about and said, 'You'll have to come and get me if you want me'. I waded through the water to her—she never moved. Then I put my hands round the back of her neck and drew her towards me, but as her face came up to mine, I smiled and then pushed her down under the water and held her there until she was dead.

"I hadn't planned on killing her that night, so I didn't have the Tarot card—the one that was supposed to be found on her body—with me. I had to take care of that little matter the next morning—in much the same way, I suspect, as you forced *The Fool* on me when I cut the cards for you a short while ago. Sleight-of-hand . . . isn't that what it's called? The quickness of the hand deceiving the eye? I simply knelt over Lorna's body—the others were standing behind me (the water was round the other side of her, and nobody was anxious to get his boots wet) : then I stole the card from inside my jacket, dropped it into my lap and then as my hand came down with the zip-fastener on her wind-cheater, I fumbled a bit, picked up the card from my lap and tossed it aside as though it had come from inside her clothing. Nobody was any the wiser."

"Feeling as you did about Lorna, it must've taken remarkable fortitude to give her the kiss of life," remarked Mrs. Charles dryly.

"Salt," he said coldly, "has, I believe, wonderful purifying properties."

"*Justice* preceding *The Moon* upright (that was the way you would've left *The Moon* on Lorna's body had you not been obliged to advance the moment of her murder) combine well. You intended her death to represent illusion—Lorna's illusions and self-deception about you—and denouncement. And the person who would bear false witness against her—which that combination of cards also predicts—was you."

"I'm almost sorry," he said, his voice faintly mocking, "that I can't allow any of this ever to be made public. I would've loved to have watched Roxeth's reaction to your denunciation of me as the Tarot murderer. Unfortunately—for you, that is—self-destruction has never held any appeal for me."

"How do you propose to stop me from telling what I know? By following me home as you did Karen Wheeler an hour or so ago and then shooting me, too?"

A sly smile stole across his face. "So that's what Merton and Sayer were doing in here!" He shook his head slowly and started to laugh. "Right under everyone's nose," he chortled softly, "the Tarot murderer

sent his final victim the first of her two cards—a combination of *The Sun* and *Death* to symbolise my (the
Tarot murderer's) radiating triumph on her death . . .
The sun, the moon and the stars," he murmured,
smiling crookedly. "That was it, the finish as far as the
Tarot murderer was concerned: only in this instance—" he frowned suddenly "—I wanted Karen to
know that she was my final victim; and so I arranged
for *The Sun* to be delivered here to her by special
messenger. I was in the crowd watching her face. She
took one look at the card and she was livid, *livid!*"
he laughed, "that I had had the gall to threaten her
when she knew so much about me."

"She was blackmailing you?"

"Threatening to. A Little Miss Nobody with big
ideas for her own rapid advancement up the social
ladder. She knew that my father was posted abroad . . .
fairly high up in the diplomatic service and likely to
go higher . . . and that there was some money about—"

"She fancied herself as the future Mrs. John Carrington-Jones?"

"That appeared to be the general idea, although
she wasn't quite the gold digger that I might've made
her seem. She was in love with me—had been ever
since we met out at one of Roxeth's parties last summer. That was her mistake. You should never be in
love with the person you intend to blackmail. You
can't mix business with pleasure."

"Karen displayed no fear when she saw a Tarot card
in the envelope that was delivered to her?"

"No. She was just angry. A lot angrier than I'd anticipated. I didn't expect that she'd leave the way she
did. She'd wanted that degrading Miss Gidding General title so badly that I couldn't imagine her walking

out on a single second of her great day of glory. Not after working so hard to get it, then losing out to Miriam and finally having it dumped in her lap.

"I started to wonder if I'd under-estimated her and she'd gone off somewhere to find a phone to tell the police what she knew—guessed, that is. I never admitted anything to her: she'd simply put two and two together . . . what she knew about Miriam and me (including the fight between Lorna and Miriam over me which she'd heard all about from Scottie), and what she knew of Lorna—they'd met, of course, out at Roxeth's—and come up with the right answer. But I was wrong, quite wrong in thinking that I'd miscalculated her moves. She wasn't looking for the nearest public telephone. Neither did she want a policeman. She went straight to her flat, which is only just around the corner from here. She didn't shut the door behind her, and I followed her inside and found her in the bathroom swallowing some headache tablets. I look care of the problem for her in a more positive way," he said with a wintry smile.

"Where did you get the gun you used to shoot her?"

"Revolver, dear lady. *Gun* indeed! It belongs to Amery Walters. He bought it some months back when his house was broken into by burglars. I stole it from the desk in his office. Tonight it will be found somewhere out at Roxeth's place . . . during the party that Roxeth is giving. Miss Gidding General was to have been one of the guests of honour . . . And Roxeth, who is well-known to make his horse-trainer's house his second home—he's always over at the stables for some reason or another—will have some pretty fast explaining to do."

He paused and eyed the clairvoyante reflectively.

"It's all worked out beautifully . . . But, you know, I was sorry about that . . . that Karen forced my hand. It was meant to happen here, after the fete was over. I'd arranged to meet her alone, to talk things over, she thought: and then someone would've found the beautiful Miss Gidding General lying dead in the bushes with all the other rubbish and litter."

He hesitated. Then, thoughtfully: "I very much regret that I never once considered the possibility that you might actually be perhaps not *cleverer*, but at least as clever as I am. You could've been my—the Tarot murderer's—*pièce de résistance*. What combination of cards would you suggest for yourself?"

"Just one card, John," she replied. "The last card in the Major Arcana."

He looked puzzled. *"The Fool?"*

"Card number twenty-one is the last picture card in the Tarot: *you* placed *The Fool* at the end of the Major Arcana and numbered it twenty-two—which is acceptable practice, although you have obviously studied the Tarot sufficiently to know that *The Fool* is an unnumbered card in the same way that the Joker in the ordinary pack of playing-cards that everyone knows has no number or suit."

"And card twenty-one is?" He smiled faintly. "You'll forgive my ignorance, Madame, but I bow before the superior knowledge of the expert and confess that you have me at a serious disadvantage."

"Yes," she said. "That, I think, could be said to be one interpretation of *The World* . . ." She smiled. "The ultimate . . . the pinnacle of attainment . . . *the card of triumph and the one towards which all others have led.*"

EPILOGUE

David Sayer sat facing Mrs. Charles across the small table in her fortune-telling booth and said, very gravely, "I think I understand, Madame, why you were reluctant to confide your suspicions about John in me. As one of James and Mary Sutherland's closest friends, it would've been a heavy burden to have had to carry around for the rest of my life—knowing, *suspecting,* that their godson had been the Tarot murderer—if you hadn't found a way of forcing him to unmask himself."

"You have spoken to Mrs. Sutherland?" the clairvoyante enquired.

He shook his head. "No, not yet. Quite frankly, I'm dreading it. Mary dotes on the boy. I'm such a coward about these things . . . I've got one of my friends out scouting around for my wife. It'll be easier, I think, if she's with me when I speak to Mary—and not just to hold Mary's hand. Mine, too! Mary's not going to forgive me for being the one who broke the bad news to her," he sighed. "It's going to scar our relationship with the Sutherlands forever. And that's a pity," he sighed again. "A great pity."

The curtain exploded suddenly and violently as Mary Sutherland burst in upon them. David got to his feet immediately and stood staring back at her, trying to think of the right words to use to begin . . .

Mary's bottom lip trembled. "David— They've taken him, *John,* away. The police . . . I just saw them. He was getting into a police car . . . What does it mean?

What's happened?" Her voice rose sharply. *"What's been going on in here this afternoon?"*

"Mrs. Sutherland," said Mrs. Charles gently. "Sit down, my dear. I have something to tell you." The clairvoyante paused and looked at David. "Superintendent . . . perhaps you would be kind enough to bring us some tea?"

AN OCCULT NOVEL OF UNSURPASSED TERROR

BY William K. Wells

Holland County was an oasis of peace and beauty . . .
    until beautiful Nicole Bannister got a horrible package that triggered a nightmare,
    until little Leslie Bannister's invisible playmate vanished and Elvida took her place,
    until Estelle Dixon's Ouija board spelled out the message: I AM COMING—SOON.

A menacing pall settled over the gracious houses and rank decay took hold of the lush woodlands. Hell had come to Holland County —to stay.

A Dell Book $2.95   (12245-7)

Dell Bestsellers